Delarosa Secrets

COLD TRUTH

T.A. CHASE

Cold Truth
ISBN # 978-1-78430-631-1
©Copyright T.A. Chase 2015
Cover Art by Posh Gosh ©Copyright May 2015
Interior text design by Claire Siemaszkiewicz
Totally Bound Publishing

Totally Bound Publishing books by T.A. Chase:

Out of Light into Darkness
From Slavery to Freedom
The Vanguard
Two for One
Where the Devil Dances
Stealing Life

The Four Horsemen
Pestilence
War
Famine
Death

The Beasor Chronicles
Gypsies
Tramps

Home
No Going Home
Home of His Own
Wishing for a Home
Leaving Home
Home Sweet Home

Every Shattered Dream
Part One
Part Two
Part Three
Part Four
Part Five

Rags to Riches Volume One
Remove the Empty Spaces
Close the Distance

Rags to Riches Volume Two
Following His Footsteps
Anywhere Tequila Flows

COLD TRUTH

Dedication

Thank you to all my readers. This wouldn't be nearly as much fun without you.

Chapter One

Taking a deep breath, Victor stopped himself from fidgeting. The head of the Delarosa cartel didn't twitch — or show any other kind of nerves — even when he was worried about the man he loved. He shoved the thought deep into the back of his mind. Victor couldn't think about love or the future. Being who he was, there wasn't a future for him unless it was in a prison cell somewhere. Yet Victor held out hope he could change the outcome.

"Señor Perez's car is at the gate," Valdez spoke from where he stood in the doorway of Victor's study.

He waved to show Valdez he'd heard him but didn't say anything as he stared out of the floor-to-ceiling windows overlooking the manicured backyard. *Can I do this? Is it possible for me to change my destiny?* Giving a full-body shake, Victor focused on what he could control.

Someone had sold him out, and he was going to hunt the person down. No one snitched to law enforcement without feeling the consequences. He was sure Bieito was already on top of that.

Stuffing his hands into his pants pockets, he frowned as one of the guards roaming the grounds walked into sight. The man was smoking and had his gun slung over his shoulder instead of in his hands. Things had gotten lax here while Victor had been in Texas. That would stop right now. He wouldn't allow any of the men to forget what their job was—protecting the compound from other cartels and the police.

He turned back to the room then picked up a pen to write a note for Bieito to call a meeting of the security unit. After that was done, he put the pen back into the drawer before pulling out a cell phone. No one knew about it, not even Bieito. He held it for a moment then returned it.

Victor tugged on his suit coat, shrugging it into position. Smoothing his hands down the front of it, he'd never admit it was to get rid of the sweat on his palms. *Christ! When did I turn into such a nervous nelly? It's not like I haven't met Bieito before.* Yet it was the first time he'd see him after Bieito had been arrested in order to keep Victor from being taken by the DEA in Houston.

I owe him so much, but how do I give him what he really wants when it would mean our deaths?

He asked that question of himself every day and hadn't been able to come up with the right answer. Maybe someday he would, and they could be happy.

Valdez fell into step behind Victor as he left the study to make his way to the front of the house. He went out onto the porch just as the black sedan pulled up.

Bieito Perez stepped from the car almost before it had stopped. He wasn't interested in waiting until the driver came around to open the door for him. There was one person he needed to see, and he knew Victor would be eager to see him as well. Straightening, he tugged on his sleeves, a nervous habit he'd tried to break several times but never figured out how.

Would Victor be angry with him for allowing himself to be arrested while Victor was spirited away? Bieito hoped his boss understood why he was willing to sacrifice his own freedom as long as Victor escaped. Lately, Victor had become unpredictable, and it was difficult to figure out exactly how the man would react to any situation.

"Perez, I'm glad you're here. Come with me." Victor motioned for him to follow.

What else was he supposed to do except go where his boss wanted him? He knew one of the servants would bring in his bag, so he entered the house, stretching his stride to keep up with Victor. Bieito dismissed Valdez with a nod before going into the study and shutting the door behind them.

Turning slowly, he braced to deal with whatever fallout might be coming his way. Victor studied him with those dark eyes, and Bieito shuddered, not hiding his reaction to that gaze. He leaned back against the door as Victor stalked toward him.

When Victor cupped his face, Bieito let his eyes drift shut and breathed. That was what he had needed ever since he'd walked out of the DEA headquarters in Houston. Victor's touch grounded him, reminding him who he belonged to and what his purpose in life was.

"Tonight you'll come to me so I can make sure nothing happened to you," Victor ordered, his lips inches away from Bieito's.

"Yes, sir," he whispered, knowing that meant him being naked and Victor fucking him. He was fine with that.

Victor rubbed his thumb across Bieito's bottom lip before stepping back. "Tell me what went on after I was spirited out of the house."

Bieito took a deep breath, used to how Victor seemed to suck the air out of the room. "Agent Jefferson put me in cuffs and tried to get me to admit to working for you."

A low growl told him Victor wasn't happy with the cuffing part. Bieito eased toward him then slipped off his suit coat, tossing it over the back of one of the chairs. He undid his cufflinks—stashing them in his shirt pocket—before rolling his sleeves up to show Victor his wrists.

"No marks. Jefferson isn't that kind of man. He's not interested in hurting me, just in arresting both of us for drug trafficking." Bieito smiled, holding up his hands.

Victor inhaled sharply and Bieito knew he was holding on to his control with the tightest grip. Yet anyone else looking at Victor would see a man who was only slightly annoyed at the inconvenience of his right-hand man being arrested.

"Wilson got there shortly after I arrived at their headquarters, though to be honest, I would've been out of there within an hour or so, even if he hadn't gotten there so quickly. The DEA doesn't have anything concrete to hold me on." He motioned to the chair and Victor nodded.

Tugging on his slacks, he took a seat then crossed his legs. If he acted like being arrested was no big deal, Victor would calm down and they could talk about everything.

"I tossed my phone right after I left. Figured the DEA—or the FBI—had put a tracker in it. Also, I got rid of everything I was wearing, which pisses me off, since that suit was one of my favorites." He whined a little. "I did grab a new tablet before I left Texas."

Victor rolled his eyes. "You can buy a new suit and put it on my account. Who do you think turned on us?"

Bieito rubbed his chin as he thought. "I'm not sure. Whoever it was is gone now, but with a little bit of research, I'll find him."

"Find him and make an example of him. No one gets away with snitching to law enforcement. I thought all of them understood that, but apparently, they need a refresher course on how to be a good cartel member." Victor paced between Bieito and his desk. "Also, I need you to send Pablo a message for me. He probably already knows, but we must inform him that we won't be back in Houston in the foreseeable future."

"Certainly, sir." He pulled his tablet out of his inside pocket then started to jot notes down. "Did Valdez do his job competently?"

Victor waved his hand in a distracted manner. "He was fine, but he's not you, and I don't like traveling without you. It must not happen again."

Bieito ducked his head to hide his pleased expression. "I'll do my damnedest to make sure it doesn't, sir. I'm glad to hear about Valdez. I've been training him to be one of your personal guards. He has potential."

"Fuck potential. I don't give a rat's ass about that," Victor muttered. "I don't want anyone protecting me except you. There's no one else I trust not to fuck me over when push comes to shove."

"I'd kill myself rather than betray you," he swore then jumped when Victor dropped to his knees in front of him. "Sir?"

Victor gripped Bieito's thighs, staring up at him with as earnest an expression as he'd ever seen on the man's face. "Don't ever say that. I don't want you to die for me, Bieito. I want us to live for each other."

Risking it, Bieito covered Victor's hands with his. "I promise I won't kill myself as long as you're still alive, but if you're dead, I won't want to continue."

Giving him a sharp nod, Victor pushed to his feet. His eyes went cold, and Bieito realized that the closeness between them was done for the moment. He scrolled through his files, checking the schedules of shipments.

"We had one larger shipment confiscated by the CBP, but it doesn't make that big a dent in our profit margin for illegals," he informed Victor.

"I wonder if the snitch told them about the shipment as well," Victor mused.

Bieito made a note to check out who knew about both. It was a short list, but there had to be some crossover. He wouldn't be happy if one of them turned out to be the informant. All the men on the list had been trusted soldiers for the cartel, and Bieito didn't like taking the time to recruit new coyotes to guide the illegals across the border.

"I'll go through the different groups," he said. "I've been hearing rumors about the CBP discovering quite a few different shipments lately. All the cartels have been hit."

"The border agents are getting better at spotting traffickers. Also, their equipment is more sophisticated. We're going to have to come up with other ways to get our product in." Victor didn't sound worried about the loss of profit.

And why would he be worried? He made millions—if not billions—of dollars every year off the addictions of others. Also, others' desperation fed his coffers, along with all of his legitimate businesses that Bieito took care of for him. Losing a few shipments here and there didn't make a dent in his money.

"Kenneth Santos," Victor said suddenly.

Frowning, Bieito looked up from the numbers he'd been studying. "Yes. What about him?"

"He's attached to the DEA agent Jefferson, isn't he?" Victor's inquiry sounded casual.

"Yes... I believe so." He wasn't sure why Victor cared, though they'd figured out Santos was related to Victor and Pablo.

Victor sighed as he crossed to look out of the windows. Bieito bit back the protest he always wanted to voice. He hated when Victor did that, because he always imagined a sniper shooting from the trees surrounding the compound. The glass wasn't bulletproof. He made a note to look into getting that kind of glass installed.

"That could be problematic," Victor commented.

Bieito agreed. "You're right. It could be, though Pablo being with Guzman hasn't caused us a problem yet."

He nodded. "Not yet, but I fear it might come to a head at some point sooner than I'm ready for."

After standing, Bieito set his tablet down then walked over to where Victor stood. He touched the small of Victor's back, knowing the gesture was hidden from view by the way Victor stood. A sense of happiness flowed through him when Victor leaned back and trusted him to take his weight for a few seconds before he straightened.

"We'll deal with it when it happens," he told Victor. "We've been through a lot and this will be one more thing to add to the list."

"Right." Victor pointed at the guard strolling through the backyard. "I saw him smoking earlier with his gun slung over his shoulder. He wasn't ready in case of an attack. They've gotten lax here with us gone all the time in Texas."

He knew what Victor wanted. "I'll gather them and remind them what they're hired to do. If I catch any of them shirking their duties again, they will be punished."

Victor eased away from him then sat at his desk. "Sit, Bieito. We need to go over the upcoming shipments and how much of each product we need to move."

"Yes, sir." He returned to his chair, picking up his tablet before he sat.

They spent the next hour discussing business, not just the cartel's but the legit ones Victor owned as well. Bieito did the accounts for all of them and made sure none of the drug money went into the other ones. Victor had family money from his mother's mother, so Bieito invested it as though he'd been thinking of Victor's retirement. Drug kingpins didn't retire. They were either arrested or they were killed by rival cartels or by their own people. Not that Bieito wanted either of those things to happen to Victor. While Victor didn't want him to sacrifice his life for Victor's, Bieito would give his last drop of blood to keep Victor safe.

"That's the last shipment you needed to decide about," he said, as he wrote down what Victor had told him to do with it. Bieito stretched then put his tablet away. His stomach growled and Victor smiled.

"Dinner should be ready by now. Let's go to the dining room." Victor gestured for him to follow, locking the door behind him once they'd stepped out.

As they strolled through the hallways, the servants greeted them with cautious smiles. Victor was a hard man, but he treated his employees well as long as they did what he ordered them. Bieito was more feared then Victor, and he did his best to keep the reputation of being the physical representation of Victor's law.

By the time they entered the dining room, the plates were set and one of the maids was placing the silverware. She bowed to Victor and him before she dashed out, heading for the kitchen.

Bieito took his usual spot on Victor's right side. He poured coffee for both of them then doctored Victor's cup just as he liked it. Victor thanked him quietly before sipping the drink. The maids brought in several dishes and bowls full of food.

Chuckling, Victor winked at Bieito. "I think they're happy to see us. I'm not sure we're going to eat all this."

"We won't, but it'll get eaten, I'm sure." He smiled at the young lady who offered him a bowl of rice.

"We'll serve ourselves," Victor dismissed them. Once they were gone, he looked over at Bieito. "I sometimes wish we could be alone all the time. Just the two of us living together, like Pablo and Mac."

Dropping his eyes, Bieito wasn't sure what to say. He'd had dreams of them like that, yet he knew the truth. Victor could get away with not being married because no one would risk pushing the head of the cartel about not having a wife. But he couldn't live as a gay man. Not in the world they were a part of.

Victor tapped his hand with his fork to get his attention. "Look at me. I'm not telling you this to hurt you. I was just talking out loud. Maybe I should keep my thoughts and wishes to myself."

"No," Bieito practically shouted. He took a deep breath, steadying his nerves. "You surprised me, is all. I want the same thing, but it hurts to hope when I know there's no way it'll come true."

He shrugged. "You might be right about that. I've come to believe there's nothing wrong with hoping, though. At times, it helps get me through the day."

Bieito studied his friend and lover. He wanted to ask what was bothering Victor, having noticed he wasn't acting like himself in the last couple of weeks. He wasn't sure Victor would tell him what was wrong, so he bit back his questions.

Victor might be more open after having sex and maybe he could find out if he needed to be worried about him.

Chapter Two

Victor heard the door open then shut, so he turned off the light in his bathroom before returning to his bedroom. Bieito stood just inside, looking unsure, and Victor hated that expression on his lover's face. After setting his drink down on the nightstand, he strolled over to Bieito, sliding his hand around the back of his head to bring their lips together.

Bieito sighed, and Victor smiled against his mouth. The man just needed to be reminded how much Victor wanted him. The way they lived during the day was difficult for both of them, though he understood it was probably even harder on Bieito than it was on him.

He caught Bieito's bottom lip between his teeth and tugged once before easing a few inches away. Bieito rested his forehead against Victor's, closing his eyes for a moment.

"I wasn't happy when you told Valdez to get me away from the house," Victor admitted.

"I know, but you can't be caught," Bieito murmured. "You can always find someone who can take my place. There's no one who can replace you."

Victor shook him a little, surprised that Bieito let Victor manhandle him like that. "I don't want to replace you. I've said this before, and you need to understand. You are *never* leaving me. You have no choice in the matter."

"Yes, sir." A smile tipped the corners of Bieito's mouth. "Will we be standing here all night or will we be moving to the bed?"

"You need to undress first," Victor ordered Bieito then turned to walk to the bed while loosening his tie. When he looked again, he caught Bieito staring at his ass. Wiggling it, he said, "Like what you see?"

Bieito snorted. "I always have, ever since I saw you when we were kids."

His soft confession hit Victor in the gut. He wished he could say he'd always known Bieito was the one for him, but that'd be a lie, and he'd sworn never to lie to his lover. What little conscience he had poked at him, and he amended what he'd thought. He would never lie to Bieito about stuff that had to do with them.

Another nudge and he heaved a mental sigh. *All right. I've lied to him about one major thing, but I'm not sure how he'll deal with it. Yet I know it's time to tell him before the issue shows up on our doorstep.*

Victor dropped to the bed, his heart heavy. The happiness and lust he'd been feeling since Bieito walked into his room faded. He stared at his feet while he thought about what he'd been doing to work out his future.

Suddenly, Bieito was there, kneeling between his legs and resting his hands on Victor's thighs. "What has you thinking so hard right now? Are you okay?"

The concerned tone of Bieito's voice brought Victor back to what they'd been about to do. His cock, which had been softening while he worried, started to stiffen again at the sight of a naked Bieito before him. He ran his fingers through Bieito's curls and smiled.

"Yes. I'm fine, love. Just got thinking." He placed a quick kiss on Bieito's lips before he could ask him about his thoughts. "We'll talk about it later."

Bieito's expression told Victor he wasn't one hundred percent convinced he was okay, but was willing to let it go for now. Victor was relieved because he really didn't want to discuss it right then. He spread his legs, urging Bieito to slide closer to him.

"Maybe you can give me something else to think about," he teased, and Bieito's eyes gleamed with determination.

Leaning back to brace his upper body, Victor watched as Bieito wrapped one of his hands around Victor's shaft then licked along the underside from base to tip. He shuddered with desire for Bieito's mouth. He wanted to demand his lover take him in, yet he knew it would be worth the wait.

Bieito pressed the tip of his tongue into Victor's slit to gather some of his pre-cum then took just the head of his cock into his mouth. Victor let his head fall back, wallowing in the heat and wetness surrounding him. He lifted his hips to push in a little more, but Bieito pressed against him to keep him from moving.

Giving up control wasn't easy for him, yet Victor trusted Bieito. There were only two other people in the entire world he loved as much as he did Bieito, but neither of them would kill—or give his life—for Victor, and that made Bieito the most important person in his life.

"Hey," he protested when Bieito let him slip from his mouth.

Chuckling, Bieito stood then grabbed Victor under his arms to move him into the middle of the bed. "Blowing you while kneeling on the floor is fine when we're in your study and someone might walk in on us. Doing it when I could be lying on a soft mattress is stupid."

He laughed as well. "You're right, though we both know no one is going to walk into my study without my permission. They're too afraid I might kill them for that sort of breach of protocol."

"Maybe not, but it's nice to pretend from time to time." Bieito leered at him as he crawled onto the covers before settling between Victor's legs again. "Ah, this is much better. I have to ask…do you want my mouth or my ass?"

Victor thought about his choices. "I want your mouth then you can have my ass."

Bieito froze, probably shocked that Victor would allow him to top. It didn't happen often, but Victor found he wanted to feel Bieito inside him. Maybe Bieito being detained by the DEA had shaken Victor more than he thought it had.

"All right." Bieito climbed off the bed.

"Where are you going?" Victor hadn't expected that reaction.

Bieito shot a grin at him over his shoulder while heading toward the bathroom. "I know how long it's been since you've had anyone in your ass. I'm going to get the lube."

He let his head drop to the pillow while he absently stroked his cock. Of course Bieito would know how long it had been because he was the only one Victor allowed to fuck him. There hadn't been another person in Victor's bed for nineteen years, since Bieito had returned from college. Victor had already begun to learn the business, and when Bieito had come home, he'd started to take over for his father as well.

Oh, he'd met many beautiful women—and handsome men—who would've been more than happy to warm his bed if he'd wanted them. He curled his lip in a sneer as he thought of them, willing to debase themselves for the power and money he had. While he might have fucked them for the night, he wouldn't have kept them around longer than that. Not when getting close to someone meant risking their lives and his.

"Got it," Bieito crowed as he stalked back into the room.

Victor watched him approach and couldn't help being amazed that such a virile man like Bieito wanted him. Bieito wasn't attracted to Victor's wealth or power. Hell, the man had enough of both without leeching off Victor. While Victor knew Bieito was afraid of him at times, it wasn't fear making him sleep with Victor either.

No. Bieito had loved him since they were children, though how a ten year old would know who he loved was beyond Victor. Being five years older than Bieito, Victor had thought the boy's love was merely hero worship, but they'd met again when Bieito had returned from Berkeley, and Victor had realized he'd been wrong.

Bieito had turned into a gorgeous man while he'd been gone, and Victor hadn't been able to deny his own attraction to his childhood friend. So he'd allowed Bieito to pursue him, doing all he could to hide it from his father along the way. Victor knew Alemando Delarosa wouldn't let his oldest son be gay, and it would've cost Bieito his life.

Taller than Victor, Bieito had broad shoulders and a narrow waist. His dark brown curls showed no sign of age, unlike Victor's own white-streaked hair. His golden skin bore the scars of his life as an enforcer, then assassin, for Victor's family. He'd heard people talk about how scary Bieito was—how cold and evil he could be. Victor never saw that. All he ever saw was the love shining in Bieito's eyes every time the man looked at him. He often wondered how other people couldn't see it.

"You're thinking too hard again," Bieito told him as he rejoined Victor on the bed. He shifted Victor around until Bieito was on his back and Victor straddled his hips. "Come up here. This way you can fuck my mouth and I can get you ready at the same time."

Riding Bieito like that was also a way for Victor to keep control of their lovemaking, and he appreciated Bieito being willing to do that for him.

Inching forward, Victor got into position, tapping Bieito's mouth with his cock. Bieito gave him a little lick, earning a growl from Victor. He heard the snap of the tube and realized Bieito wasn't going to start sucking him until he got his fingers coated.

He held Bieito's gaze then jumped when Bieito's slick-covered fingers trailed along his crease to rub over his hole. Bieito gave him a wicked grin then opened his mouth to let Victor fill him. After taking the cue, Victor eased forward by bracing his hands on the headboard in front of him and rocking his hips back and forth.

Bieito didn't fight him, just relaxed his throat and let Victor fuck his face. The suction he applied to Victor's shaft caused Victor to groan. Then Bieito pressed the tip of one finger in as Victor moved back.

He tensed at the invasion, but Bieito didn't try to go farther, letting Victor do everything. Once his body had accepted the intrusion, he exhaled and relaxed. Bieito hummed in encouragement as he began moving again. Back and forth. In and out.

"Christ! I love your mouth and your touch," he muttered, his gaze locked with Bieito's.

He was so distracted by Bieito's tongue, licking and teasing his length, he never noticed when his lover had worked three fingers in until Bieito managed to hit his gland with his knuckle.

"Fuck!" he shouted and jerked.

Bieito pinched his hip with his other hand, and Victor reached down to run his fingers over Bieito's hollowed cheeks in apology. His balls drew up to his body and the pressure built in his groin.

"I'm going to come," he warned Bieito, who sped up the fingering and swallowed around Victor's shaft.

When his climax hit him, he cried out as he flooded Bieito's mouth. His lover drank his cum down, though a little slipped from the corner of his lips. He slumped over and that was the signal Bieito must have been waiting for, because he let Victor slide out then gripped his hips.

"Can I?" he asked, and Victor nodded, rocking back and impaling himself on Bieito's cock. "It won't be long."

Victor didn't think it would. Watching him come always put Bieito on edge and with a quick slam down, he took him all the way in. Victor rocked in counterpoint to each of Bieito's thrusts. They'd been making love for so many years that he knew exactly how to move to drive Bieito crazy. Sweat dripped from Victor's chin to trickle along Bieito's chest. When Bieito lost the smooth rhythm of his strokes, it was time. He clenched his inner muscles around Bieito and the man yelled out his name as he came, filling Victor's ass with heat.

He collapsed into Bieito's embrace and they trembled together, panting while trying to calm their hearts. Victor didn't protest when Bieito gently rolled him onto his back then climbed from the bed.

As Victor stared up at the ceiling, his mind was blank and he liked it that way. Throughout the day, he always had to be on his toes, keeping his eyes open for danger and treachery coming at him from every direction. Yet here in his bedroom, with Bieito in the bathroom, Victor could let down his guard and simply breathe, existing only for the man he loved.

The mattress dipped, and he turned his head to see Bieito kneeling on it, a washcloth in his hand. Victor didn't say anything as Bieito cleaned him up then pitched the cloth back toward the bathroom. He crawled under the blankets when Bieito lifted them.

He settled into Bieito's arms, knowing he wouldn't be there in the morning when Victor woke. Bieito never spent the night. They couldn't risk someone finding them in bed together.

"Someday," he whispered, "we'll be able to wake up in each other's arms."

"It's a wonderful dream," Bieito murmured in his ear, pulling him tightly against his side. "Will you tell me what's been bothering you lately?" He seemed hesitant to ask.

Victor sighed, not wanting to destroy the joyful emotions he felt, but knowing he needed to tell Bieito the whole truth. Yet before he could say a word, someone pounded on his door.

"Señor Delarosa, there's someone here to see you," Valdez shouted through the door. "I'm sorry to bother you, but I couldn't find Señor Perez anywhere."

"Shit," Bieito muttered. "I'll grab my stuff and hide in the bathroom. You get dressed and go with him. I'll join you as soon as I can."

Victor sprang from their bed. "Who is it, Valdez?"

"She wouldn't give us her name. Just kept saying it had something to do with Kemen. Said you would know what she meant." Valdez sounded slightly freaked, as though having to deal with a hysterical woman wasn't his area of expertise.

"Kemen?" Victor dragged his clothes on, not caring how he looked. All that mattered was getting to Esperanza as quickly as possible. He shot Bieito a glance. "Come to me as soon as you can. This is vitally important."

Bieito nodded, though Victor could see his confusion. He didn't have time to explain, but he knew Bieito would be there as soon as he could sneak out of Victor's room.

After pressing a hard kiss to Bieito's lips, Victor shoved his feet into a pair of running shoes then slid out of the door, making sure Valdez couldn't get a look into the room.

"Take me to her at once," he demanded.

"Yes, Señor." Valdez whirled, obviously sensing the urgency. "I wouldn't have bothered you, but as I said, I couldn't find Señor Perez."

"I'm sure he'll show up as soon as he's aware we have a visitor. How did she look?"

Valdez lifted one shoulder. "She is very distraught, Señor. I don't know who this Kemen is, but it's clear she cares for him a great deal."

Victor wanted to tell Valdez that he cared about Kemen as well, but caught himself. He couldn't tell a simple employee about his son before he told the man he loved.

Chapter Three

Mac and Snap stood under the oak tree while Tanner and Ken sat at the picnic table watching them. Ken and Snap had come over for dinner, and Tanner studied his half-brother.

"You're looking much better than when I saw you in the hospital," he told Ken.

Ken chuckled. "I'm feeling better too. That was a rough couple of hours. Snap told him that an informant called him with my whereabouts."

Tanner pursed his lips, not sure how much he should say. Mac hadn't told him how they'd gotten the information, and to be honest, Tanner hadn't asked. He didn't want to know exactly how Victor had ensured Snap found Ken. All he knew was that it had been done.

Eyeing him, Ken asked, "Did our big brother have anything to do with my rescue?"

"He might have. I really can't say for sure." Tanner tapped his fingers on the top of the table. "I try very hard not to know anything about him, in case I'm asked. It also is easier for Mac as well."

"Makes sense." Ken turned his gaze back to Snap and Mac. "We haven't discussed the family situation that much."

Snorting, Tanner gave Ken an understanding look. "I try not to talk about him either. It's easier."

Their partners joined them, and Tanner noticed both of them looked concerned. He leaned against Mac then poked him in the side.

"What's wrong with you two?"

Mac looked over at Snap, who shrugged. Ken edged closer to Snap, wrapping his arm around the big man's waist.

"Snap got some news from an agent friend of his who's working with the police down in Mexico. They're gathering information and evidence against the cartels."

Tanner stiffened, but Mac shook his head. "Don't worry about something you have no control over."

"What he told me was about Victor, but not about them arresting him or anything like that," Snap spoke up then he took a deep breath. "My friend's been hearing rumors that the Cortez cartel is planning to make a move on Victor."

"A move? Does that mean they're going to kill him or try to take over his territory?" Ken sounded distressed, which surprised Tanner since he knew Ken wasn't entirely convinced about Victor.

Both Mac and Snap shook their heads. After Tanner stood, he went inside to grab the steaks they were going to grill. He braced his hands on the counter in the kitchen and let his head drop forward. *Christ!* He wanted to snatch up his phone and call Victor, but he wouldn't be able to get a hold of him. His brother was in Mexico and never contacted Tanner while he was there.

"Come on outside," Mac said from where he leaned in the doorway. "We're going to spend time with our family."

Tanner handed him the plate of meat before he got the potatoes and salad. When they got back outside, Ken was talking softly with Snap.

"Tanner," Snap addressed him.

"Yes?" He set the food on the table then met Snap's gaze.

"My friend wasn't sure what was going on. Just that there was a shake-up happening. They're keeping an eye on the situation because they don't want it spiraling out of control and hurting civilians. He promised me he'd get a hold of me if they discover anything concrete."

He nodded. "Thanks, Snap. I know you don't like thinking about who our brother is, but he's still family to me and I do care about him."

Snap reached over to grip his hand. "I get it, Tanner. No matter who our family is, we still love them. Sometimes they make it harder than other times."

That was true. He grinned at Snap before wandering over to check on Mac, who was getting the grill ready. Mac pulled him close for a quick kiss, and Tanner took a moment to remember he had a man who loved him more than anything else in the world. Plus, he had friends who knew his deepest secret but chose to care about him anyway.

He'd worry quietly about Victor and pray nothing happened to his brother.

* * * *

Victor followed closely behind Valdez. When the man pointed to the main reception room where guests were always placed, he shot past him into the room.

"Esperanza," he exclaimed.

The petite, dark-haired woman shot up from where she'd been sitting then raced into his arms. "Victor, they took Kemen."

He wrapped her tight to his chest then brushed a kiss over her hair. "Who took him?"

"I don't know. He was at a café with some friends and a black truck stopped near them. Then these armed gunmen jumped out and forced Kemen into the vehicle with them." She peered up at him, her eyes bloodshot and swollen from crying. "I know I said I would never bother you, but I didn't know who else to turn to."

"No. You did the right thing," he told her, leading her back to the couch then easing her down. "Please sit."

She clung to him but did as he'd said. He dropped next to her, fear coursing through his body. He'd never felt this afraid, not even when his father had attacked him and forced him to fight back.

"Señor Delarosa?" Valdez sounded hesitant, as though he was really unsure about what to do.

"Valdez, go and wake one of the maids. Have her get the White Room ready for Señor Delarosa's visitor. Then get the cook up and have her make some tea and sandwiches. I have no doubt the lady hasn't eaten in quite some time." Bieito stalked into the room, dressed as though he'd been outside on a run.

"I tried to find you, Señor, but you weren't in your room," Valdez pointed out, obviously not wanting to get in trouble for not informing his boss about their visitor.

Bieito dismissed his concern with a wave of his hand. "I couldn't sleep, so I went for a run. Now go and do as I told you. When you're done, you can go back to your post by the front door."

Victor met Bieito's gaze but saw nothing there. His expression was blank, as it often was when there were other people in the room with them.

"Yes, Señor." Valdez left them alone.

Esperanza had hid her face in Victor's shoulder, sobbing and soaking his shirt. Victor rubbed her back with one hand while gesturing to the side bar with the other. Bieito nodded before going over to pour out a small amount of whiskey. He brought the glass to Victor then after handing it to him, Bieito moved to stand by the door.

"I'll leave you to talk, sir."

Bieito started to leave, but Victor shook his head. "No. You—of all people—should hear what Esperanza has to say. Plus, I'm going to need your help with this."

He could tell Bieito wasn't happy about being asked to stay. Victor was pretty sure it had to do with the rather familiar way he was holding Esperanza, yet Victor wasn't about to abandon her. Not now, when her worst fear had come true.

"Come and sit," he said, nodding toward the chair across from him. "This isn't how I wanted to tell you."

"Tell me what?" Bieito edged closer to the chair but didn't sit. He clasped his hands behind his back and spread his feet. Victor called it his bodyguard stance, and it was plain to see that Bieito wasn't Victor's lover at the moment. He was the man who'd been trained to protect Victor from any kind of danger. Bieito had no way to know that Esperanza didn't represent any danger to him.

"Victor, what are we going to do? They'll kill him if they know Kemen's your son," she spoke up.

Bieito's eyes widened, and Victor saw a flash of hurt in them before they went flat and cold. "Your son?"

"Kemen is twenty years old and a junior at the university in Mexico City," Victor explained. "I was going to tell you tonight before Valdez interrupted us. I was afraid something like this would happen."

"Something like your son being kidnapped off the streets of Mexico City? Something that could've been prevented if I had known you had a son?" Bieito didn't raise his voice and, in a way, that was worse than if he had shouted those words at Victor.

Esperanza must have sensed the tension between the two of them because she pushed away from Victor to glare at Bieito. "Who are you to talk to him like that? He is your employer. You have no right to question him."

Victor squeezed her hand. "That's not true, Espe. Bieito has every right to be angry with me."

"No," Bieito broke in. "She's right. I'm just your personal assistant. I have no right to be upset with you about what has gone on in your past. I need all the information you can give me, Señora. Once I have everything, I'll start the search for your son."

He wanted to get up and punch Bieito as hard as he could in the face. How dare he act as though he were nothing to Victor except a servant? Yet the knowledge that Victor had a son would be hard for Bieito to deal with all at once—he had to allow Bieito to process the information in his own way, but unfortunately, they didn't have the time for that.

"Esperanza and I met when I was away at college. We fell in love and she got pregnant. Kemen was born shortly before my father called me back home." Victor glanced down at the beautiful lady next to him. "She knew who I was and didn't want to have anything to do with the family business."

"I didn't want my son to grow up to be a drug lord. I want Kemen to be an honest man," she said. "A man his mother could be proud of."

He tried not to wince. His own mother had left him behind when she couldn't take being married to Alemando Delarosa any more. She'd taken Victor's younger brother, Pablo, with her, changing their names when they'd gotten into the US.

Victor hadn't been shocked when Esperanza had told him she wanted nothing to do with him or the cartel. He'd honored her wishes, not telling anyone about Kemen's existence, not even the man he'd grown to love.

Bieito opened his mouth then seemed to change his mind about what he was going to say. "You've been living in the capital ever since then?"

She nodded. "Yes. Victor bought us a nice house and paid our bills. When the time came for Kemen to go to the university, Victor paid for that as well. I have never spoken of him to Kemen, not wanting him to be ashamed of his father."

Victor saw Bieito tense, and he could almost hear him gritting his teeth. He cleared his throat. "Esperanza, we need to know the names of Kemen's friends who were with him at the café. Also, did he ever say anything about being followed or approached by anyone before?"

Bieito went back to the doorway then crouched next to a small bag on the floor. Victor hadn't seen him carry it in, but it was no surprise since Bieito believed in being prepared for everything.

By the time he'd returned to his chair with his ever-present tablet, one of the maids was wheeling in a cart with a tea set on it. There was also a plate of empanadas. Victor fixed Esperanza a cup then put some food on a small plate for her. She thanked him and he smiled at her, though every atom in his body wanted to yell at her to hurry and tell them what they needed to know.

They had to find Kemen before the men who had him made an example of him. Victor was afraid he knew exactly who'd taken his son, and when he found them, he would kill each and every one.

"Señora, your son's friends," Bieito reminded her.

"Right." She gave him the names of four young men who had been with Kemen at the time of the kidnapping. In addition to that, she told him the name of the café and several other places Kemen liked to hang out when he wasn't in class.

By the time she was done recounting Kemen's daily activities, she was plainly exhausted. She was pale with dark circles under her eyes and her hands shook. Victor stood then went to ring for a maid.

"Espe, dear, I'm going to have one of my maids take you up to your room. There will be clothes for you to change into. Why don't you take a nice bath and try to get some sleep? I promise you, Perez and I will leave for Mexico City right away. We'll have Kemen back to you in no time." Victor took her hand and helped her off the couch.

"I knew you'd be able to help me, Victor." She hugged him. "I'm not going to be able to sleep a wink until Kemen is returned to me."

He returned her hug. "At least try to rest."

The maid entered and Victor led Esperanza over to her. "Rosita, take Señora Larenz to the White Room.

Make sure she has everything she needs to be comfortable for the night."

"Yes, Señor." Rosita gestured for Esperanza to come with her.

Once the women were out of the room, Victor stalked over to the side bar then poured himself a shot of whiskey before drinking it down. He slammed the empty glass onto the top and swore.

"God damn it."

Whirling, he threw the glass against the opposite wall, listening to it shatter just like his heart. Having her sons kidnapped had been his mother's worst fear. It was why she'd ended up leaving his father, in the end. Victor thought he'd escaped that threat because he'd never claimed Kemen as his.

"Throwing things isn't going to fix this situation," Bieito spoke from where he still sat, typing things into his tablet and not looking at him.

"Maybe not, but it makes me feel better. I'll kill them all when we find them," he vowed.

"I have no doubt about that, but first you need to go back to bed." Bieito entered one last thing then stood, holding the tablet by his side.

Victor shook his head. "I'm not going to be shuffled off to bed like a child."

Bieito shrugged. "You're going to need your rest, sir. We'll be leaving first thing in the morning for the capital. I'll be up most of the night contacting our men in the city and getting them organized. As much as I'd like for you to stay here, I know better than to think you'll listen to me. We'll be traveling fast and light, sir, and we can't have you slowing us down."

He shot across the room, all his anger and fear making him hate Bieito's calm expression. After drawing back his arm, he punched Bieito directly in the face. The moment his fist connected with Bieito's chin, some of Victor's anger dissipated, but what was done was done, and he couldn't take it back.

Chapter Four

Bieito knew the punch was coming, and while he could've avoided it, he also knew Victor needed an outlet for his rage and fear. Since fucking Bieito was out of the question at that moment, hitting him was probably the next best thing.

When Victor drew his arm back to hit him again, Bieito caught his fist in his hand. "If you ever got angry and threw punches, I'd take a beating to make you feel better, but you don't do things like this. You have to get yourself under control, sir. This isn't going to get your son back any sooner."

What he really wanted to do was wrap his arms around Victor and hold him close. Unfortunately, just like they didn't have time for Victor to beat the shit out of him, they didn't have the time for him to comfort his lover.

"Fuck you, Bieito. Why are you so calm about this whole thing?" Victor jerked his hand away from his grip then whirled to pace around the room.

"I'm calm because that's what you and Kemen need right now. Maybe once you have him back, I'll get upset and curse at you. Not right now."

He meant it. Bieito was good at compartmentalizing. Pushing all his emotions about finding out about Kemen into a small box in the back of his mind was easy for him. There were other things that needed his attention right now. No matter what his feelings were, Bieito wasn't going to let Kemen stay in the enemies' hands for any longer than necessary.

"I do have one question though," he stated.

"What?" Victor glared at him.

"Are there any other children we need to be worried about? I need to know if I have to send men out to protect them." Bieito rubbed his aching chin while he tried to figure out how many men he trusted enough to place as bodyguards if Victor had more kids out there.

Victor shook his head. "There aren't any more out there, Bieito. Esperanza was the only girl I slept with who ever got pregnant. Once you came back home, there's been no one else."

His shoulders relaxed as he let that worry go. Now he could focus on getting Kemen away from whoever had him. After that, they'd work out what to do. Bieito realized Victor had probably spent a lot of time trying to keep Kemen from this life, not because he was ashamed as Esperanza seemed to be of what Victor did. He was pretty sure Victor had kept Kemen in the dark in hopes that the young man would be safe.

"Good. Then I won't have to split our forces. Now please, sir, go and try to lie down. I know you probably won't sleep." Bieito shrugged. "I need to start getting things rolling."

Victor studied him. "Do you think I won't be any use to you? Is that why you're sending me away?"

Sighing, Bieito stepped closer to him and took a risk by cupping Victor's face in his hands then kissing him. He felt Victor relax a little before he eased his mouth a few inches away. "You're going to be a lot of help once we get to the city and figure out what the fuck is going on, but you don't need to be here while I get the mission in order. You like to do things. There's not a lot of *doing* right now—just a lot of calling and arranging."

His dark eyes stared into Bieito's, and Bieito could see how much reassurance Victor needed that they'd get Kemen back before anything bad happened. Bieito wished he was the kind of person who could lie to the man he loved. Yet he knew Victor would be furious if he did, so he kissed him again then stepped back.

"If you can't sleep and need something to do, then go get me some coffee. It's going to be a long night, and I haven't had much sleep yet." He managed to wink and Victor gave him a small smile.

"I can do that." He touched Bieito's chin and whispered, "I'm sorry."

Before he could say anything, Victor left. Bieito sat on the couch, braced his elbows on his knees then let his head drop into his hands. He only took a moment to think about how much his heart hurt because of Victor keeping Kemen a secret from him. Then he pushed it into another box in his brain.

Climbing to his feet, he dusted his hands off as though he were wiping away any unhappy thoughts. It was time get the rescue mission started then he would figure out whom he would have to kill for this.

He pulled out his tablet, scrolling through the list of names in the capital. When he got to the head of the

Mexico City branch of the Delarosa cartel, he grunted. Bieito dug out his phone, dialing the man's number.

"Jorge," he said when the man answered.

"Yes, boss?" Jorge sounded as though Bieito had woken him, which was probably true.

"Get your ass out of bed. We have an emergency. A young man named Kemen Larenz has been kidnapped, probably earlier yesterday or maybe the day before. I need you to get your men looking for any information they can find on him and who took him," he ordered.

Jorge mumbled something, but Bieito chose to ignore it. He didn't care whether Jorge complained about having to get up or not. He simply wanted the man to do it.

"Why are we looking for this man?" Jorge asked.

Bieito growled before saying, "Do you really think it's any of your business why I want the information? Just get it for me, Jorge, or I'll find someone who will."

There was no hesitation in his voice, and he knew Jorge understood what he was saying. He would find someone to replace Jorge then kill him to make a point. When they questioned him, they were questioning Victor by proxy, and Bieito wouldn't allow that.

"Sorry, boss," Jorge apologized.

"Just get the information. Señor Delarosa and I will be in the city by ten in the morning. I'll expect you to be ready to give us a report as soon as we arrive," Bieito snapped.

"Yes, sir. Certainly, sir. Do you need me to arrange for any additional guards while you're here?" Jorge finally sounded like he was awake.

Bieito thought about it for a moment. "No. We'll be bringing our own men."

Jorge was silent for a second, but Bieito didn't care what the man was thinking. He wasn't going to risk Victor's safety by using men they didn't know for protection. He knew the men at the compound—had trained them himself—and he trusted them as much as he trusted anyone at the moment.

"I understand. If we find out where the young man is being kept, do you want us to rescue him or do we wait?" It was obvious Jorge knew Bieito didn't trust him, but again, Bieito didn't care.

"No. If you manage to find out where he's at, you'll make note of it then let me know. I want nothing to be done until we're there." He glanced up to see Victor walking in, carrying a carafe and two mugs. Apparently, he wasn't going to be alone the rest of the night if the second cup was any indication. "Do you understand me, Jorge?"

Jorge grunted then said, "Yes, sir. I'll get my men out looking to see what they can discover. I'll be waiting for your call in the morning."

"Good." Bieito hung up before taking the coffee Victor handed him. He drank the whole cup, burning his tongue, but hoping the caffeine would hit him quickly.

Victor joined him on the couch, leaning into his side. Bieito wanted to wrap his arm around Victor's shoulders to try to comfort him, but he didn't know if someone might walk in on them, and he couldn't have Victor show any weakness in front of his men.

"I have Jorge putting boots on the streets and gathering any kind of intel he can on Kemen or who might have him," he informed Victor.

"I think we both know who has my son, Bieito," Victor said, staring into his own mug.

Bieito hummed, not wanting to put a name to their enemy, even though they both knew there could only be one person who would dare to kidnap a Delarosa. "How did he know Kemen was your son when no one else does?"

Pursing his lips, Victor turned to look at him. "That's a good question. I think we might want to wake Esperanza up and see who she's been seeing lately."

"You don't keep track of that?" He was shocked, since Victor kept track of every move Pablo and Mac made all the way up in Houston.

"Not hers. I kept a distant eye on Kemen, but now I know I should've told you about him." Victor pushed to his feet.

As much as Bieito wanted to say 'yes, you should've told me a long time ago', he didn't. It wasn't his place right then to yell or get angry with Victor about lying to him. They all had their secrets and, in a way, he could understand why Victor had never said a word about having a child.

"If you had known, he wouldn't have been taken. You would've made sure he had guards at all times, and he would've never seen them if I didn't want him to." Victor rested his hand on Bieito's shoulder. "You've done it for years with Pablo, and it's one of the many things I appreciate that you do for me."

Not words of love, yet he understood it was the closest Victor could bring himself to saying he loved Bieito. He'd take them for right now, knowing there would be a time when he would want to hear something different to keep his heart from breaking.

"Protecting Pablo is my job, as much as protecting you is. Serving the Delarosa family has been the Perez family's duty for generations." Bieito met Victor's gaze. "Though it's not just duty that keeps me here."

Victor's grip tightened, and he nodded before he strolled away. Bieito stood as well, going out into the hallway to see who was at the front door. Rodriguez sat in a chair out of sight from the windows in the door, machine gun across his lap.

"Rodriguez, were you on duty when Señora Larenz arrived?" he asked, as he approached the guard.

After standing, Rodriguez shook his head. "No, boss. I had about ten minutes before my shift started. Valdez called me to come over early because he needed to deal with something. When I got to the porch, a car was parked in front, and Valdez was talking to the lady."

Bieito had his tablet out to take notes while the man talked to him. "Is the car still here?"

"Yes, though Valdez had Guillermo pull it around to the visitor's garage." Rodriguez bit his bottom lip, and Bieito knew he was nervous, not sure why Bieito was questioning him.

"Get on the radio and tell Valdez I need him in the study as soon as he can get here. He needs to find someone to take his place. I need Guillermo to write down the license number from the car and bring it to me as well."

Rodriguez's eyes widened, but he did as Bieito had told him. Bieito went back into the study to find Victor staring up at the picture of his mother hanging over the fireplace.

"The maid is bringing Esperanza down for us to talk to," Victor told him.

He gritted his teeth at the thought of having to deal with the woman—not only because she was the mother of Victor's only son, but because she seemed to look down on Victor for what he did for a living. While being the head of a cartel didn't hold the same prestige as being a rock star or the president, Victor was still an important person and deserved Esperanza's respect.

"I'll talk to her. You just stand behind me and look menacing." Victor flashed him a smile. "I know you weren't happy with her while she was talking earlier."

"She acts as though she's ashamed of you," Bieito informed him. "I'm sure you've been supporting her since you returned to the compound. You're paying for Kemen's education as well. She has no right to treat you like dirt."

He frowned as Victor chuckled and walked over to him. Bieito accepted Victor's touch on his cheek, nuzzling his palm for a quick second.

"You are the only person in the world who sees me not as the monster I am, but as a good man worth loving." Victor stared at him with a certain amount of awe in his eyes. "I've never been able to figure out how I got so lucky as to find a man like you."

Bieito snorted. "I know exactly the kind of man you are, Victor. I also know how much being that man has cost you. I've killed men. Does knowing that make you unable to look at me? Does it disgust you?"

Victor shook his head. "Considering you killed them on my orders, no. It doesn't disgust me at all."

Before they could say anything else, a shrill voice came from outside the study.

"I'm perfectly capable of walking. Get your hands off me. Victor will have your job when he finds out about this," Esperanza shrieked as she stalked into the room.

Valdez followed her, rolling his eyes when he met Bieito's gaze. "I have the information you asked for, boss." He held out a small piece of paper.

"Thank you." Glancing over to Victor, he said, "I need to go talk to Valdez."

Nodding, Victor eyed Esperanza. "That's fine. Return when you're done. I'll chat with our lovely guest."

The tone of his voice caused her to pale, and Bieito couldn't help the little leap of joy his heart did at the thought of her being afraid of Victor. She should be, especially if she was the reason why Kemen had been taken.

Bieito turned back to Valdez. "Let's go into my office."

"Yes, boss." Valdez bowed slightly to Victor before heading toward the room just off Victor's study, where Bieito did all the cartel's business.

He heard Esperanza inhale sharply, and he wondered if she was going to ask them to stay. Like he'd go against what Victor had told him.

After leaving the door between the rooms open a few inches, he gestured for Valdez to sit. The man looked nervous, but Bieito wasn't angry with him. He just needed some more details about Esperanza's arrival at the compound. He sat at his desk then turned on his computer. While he waited for it to wake up, he looked at Valdez.

"Tell me what happened when Señora Larenz arrived."

Valdez took a deep breath, and Bieito was sure he was about to make some kind of apology or excuse. He held up his hand.

"I'm not angry—or upset—with you, Valdez. I'm simply gathering everything I can about what has been going on."

His employee relaxed and Bieito motioned for him to start again.

Chapter Five

Victor pointed at the couch. "I think you should sit, Esperanza. I'd like to have a serious talk with you."

She flounced over then sat, looking gorgeous in her black silk robe that gaped at her chest, revealing her ample cleavage. Those weren't her natural breasts, and he should know since he'd been intimately acquainted with them at one time. Folding her hands in her lap, she met his gaze and he could see fear in her eyes.

"What's the meaning of this, Victor? Do you know how upset I've been since Kemen was taken? I'd finally managed to fall asleep and your maid woke me." She pouted.

He was unaffected by her plump lips and her worried mother routine. While he had loved her at one time, he'd never really trusted her. Hell, there was only person in the entire world he trusted to not screw him over and he was in the other room. Victor had always known Esperanza would do something to take advantage of her connection with him, whether she actually wanted him around or not.

"One of the questions that keeps popping up while we look into this kidnapping is how did whoever took Kemen know he was important. I've done everything you wanted and stayed away from my son because you didn't want him to know his father was a Delarosa." He paced in front of her, hands hanging loosely at his sides, seemingly relaxed and simply curious.

She shrugged as though clueless, yet he saw her fidget with the edge of her robe as well. There was something she wasn't telling him. Something he was pretty sure would piss him off when he found out what it was.

The house phone rang before he could ask her another question. They both stiffened and he heard Bieito answer it. There were a few clipped sentences then silence. He watched as the door between their offices was nearly ripped off its hinges and Bieito stalked in.

"The phone is for you, sir," Bieito told him. His voice held rage, and Victor could see that same emotion burning in Bieito's eyes.

"Who is it?" He headed to his desk.

"I'm not sure which bastard he belongs to, but he's calling about Kemen." Bieito turned back to his office. "Valdez, I want you to hand-pick ten men to come with us to Mexico City. You must be ready to go by six. Also, pack the assault equipment."

Valdez, who had trailed behind Bieito, blinked at his barked orders, but didn't argue. "Yes, boss. I'll pick my ten best."

"Men you trust to protect Señor Delarosa with their lives. Because if they don't, I'll kill them myself." Bieito snarled.

"Of course." Valdez dashed from the room.

Victor picked up the receiver then punched the button for line one. "Delarosa." He kept his tone unbothered. No one was to know how angry he was. Not yet. The time would come when he could unleash all of his hatred, but it wasn't right then.

"We have something you want, Delarosa. If you wish to see him alive again, you need to listen closely to what I'm going to say."

He shot Bieito a glance and got a nod in return. He should've known Bieito was trying to trace the call.

"Exactly who are you talking about? I'm not missing anything important."

Esperanza gave a little scream, prompting Bieito to go over and clap his hand over her mouth. Victor winced slightly at the squeak she gave. Bieito didn't use the softest touch.

"Nice try, Victor. We know he's your son and if you care for him at all, you'll do as I say."

"You will address me as Señor Delarosa," Victor said coldly. "I'm not your friend or relation to be treated so familiarly. Tell me your demands."

There was an audible swallow from the man on the other end of the phone call. Victor sneered at the knowledge he was scared of Victor, even though they weren't in the same room.

"I'll find out who you are, and when I do, your days will be numbered. Your blood will coat my hands when I slit your throat," he threatened, yet it was a promise as well. He never said things like that without meaning them.

A threat was only as good as the intent behind it. If a person understood he meant exactly what he threatened, then they were more likely to do what he wanted to keep from enduring what he'd vowed would happen to them.

The man whimpered and Victor wondered if he'd just pissed himself.

"Get on with the conditions. As soon as I hang up, I'll be hunting you. Maybe you should just abandon whomever you work for and get out of the country." He snorted softly. "Though that won't keep you safe."

He dug out a pen and some paper to write down the directions as the man babbled. A low growl filled the room, causing him to glance over to where Bieito stood next to Esperanza, no longer covering her mouth. Her robe had fallen off one shoulder, and Bieito was staring down at her flesh. She gave him a weakly flirtatious smile.

Victor wanted to tell her that it wouldn't work on Bieito. The man had never shown any inclination to bed a woman. Oh, he could appreciate a beautiful lady as much as the next man. He just never wanted to sleep with them—or at least Victor had never known him to take a woman to his bed.

"Exactly how long do I have to gather the money?" He returned his attention to the phone conversation.

"You have three days. At the end of that time, you'll receive another phone call with instructions on how you are to deliver the ransom." The man hung up and Victor slammed the receiver back into the cradle of the phone.

"God damn," he cursed. "The mother fuckers want six million dollars in American currency for Kemen."

"Non-sequential bills?" Bieito asked, not moving from where he loomed over Esperanza.

"Of course." He stalked around his desk then went right to Esperanza. "How the hell did anyone find out who Kemen was?"

She started to shake her head, but he grabbed her chin to keep her from doing so. He squeezed just a little. Her wince told him she would probably have bruises there in the morning.

"Don't tell me you have no idea, my dear. I think you know exactly who told them about my son. I think you bragged to the wrong lover, and they went running to Cortez with the information." He shook her slightly before letting go of her to begin pacing again.

She went to jump to her feet, and Bieito pushed her back down. If looks could kill, she'd have murdered him right there, yet Bieito seemed unconcerned about her indignation at his treating her like that.

"Answer Señor Delarosa's question," Bieito demanded, his voice menacing.

"I'd never betray you like that, Victor. I've kept my part of our agreement," Esperanza protested.

He swung back to face her. "It was the American movie star you've been fucking over the last year, wasn't it?"

"Mitch would never do that. He loves me," she cried.

"He loves his drugs first and foremost. Mitchell Manchester is an addict, and while he might like fucking you, he'll sell his soul for cocaine." Victor rubbed his hands together and couldn't help but laugh at her surprised expression. "Did you think I wouldn't investigate any man you brought around Kemen? Even with him being at university, he would still interact with your lover, and I wanted to make sure he wouldn't be too bad of an influence on him."

Esperanza seemed to fold into herself. "Why would he tell them about Kemen's connection with you?"

Bieito tapped her on the top of the head lightly. "If I remember correctly, he owes the Cortez cartel a great deal of money. He's been getting his drugs on credit, and they must have called his IOU due."

Victor had forgotten he'd asked Bieito to dig through Manchester's background and financials, though he hadn't said why he wanted it done. "I told my dealers not to sell to him."

"Like they would listen to you," she scoffed. "You drug dealers will take money from a child."

He couldn't argue that point. "I don't allow my dealers to give drugs out on credit. If I find out they have, they only get one chance to correct the situation before they are disciplined."

Her wince told him she was imagining just what kind of punishment they received. He went to stand in front of her, forcing her to look up at him.

"Did you tell Manchester who Kemen's father was, Esperanza? You need to tell me the truth. You know what will happen if you don't." He clenched his hands and her eyes widened.

"You're a monster, Victor Delarosa. Have you no morals? Do you get off on scaring women into doing what you want?" she screamed.

He'd heard all of it before. There was nothing Esperanza could shout at him that hadn't been said at some point in his life. His self-esteem would be shot if he listened to all the vitriol people spouted at and about him. There was a soft snort and he looked up to see Bieito roll his eyes.

As much as he wanted to laugh, he managed to keep his lips from twitching. Victor met her gaze and didn't look away, putting on his fiercest expression. She obviously thought he wouldn't hit her, but if doing that would give him a chance to save his son, he'd do what he had to do.

"Of course, you'd have no qualms about torturing me to get what you think is the truth," she railed. "You sell drugs for a living. You have no soul."

"Esperanza," was all he said, and she froze. He leaned in close. "Tell me what I want to know, or it won't be me getting the information from you." He let his gaze skate over to where Bieito stood, arms folded and eyes narrowed.

Esperanza whimpered then said, "All right. Yes, I told Mitch you were Kemen's father." Both he and Bieito snarled, and she started sobbing. "He said he loved me, and I didn't want to have any secrets between us. I didn't know what he was going to do with the information."

"Bullshit. You had to have known he was an addict, Señora." Bieito edged closer. "His need for the coke is so strong, he would sell his soul for it, which is what he did."

"He told me it was just a casual thing. He only did it when he needed a boost for a movie shoot or something," she mumbled.

Victor sighed. "Cocaine is never casual. He lied. Manchester owes so much money to the Cortez cartel that he had to find a way to expunge his debt. The only way he could do that was by telling them about Kemen. You endangered your son's life because you wanted to keep your younger lover in your bed."

She leaped to her feet and would've slapped him if Bieito hadn't caught her hand. He shoved her back down then stood right next to her. Victor hadn't moved an inch. There was no way she intimidated him. He'd been hit by his father, who hadn't pulled any of his strength just because Victor was his son.

"I endangered *your* son?" Esperanza screamed, and he barely stopped himself from wincing at the shrillness of her voice. "You've done nothing for him in the twenty years he's been alive. I'm the one who took care of him all those years. I was the one who made sure he was fed and clothed. I had to put my life on hold until he went away for college."

"Stop laying it on so thick, my dear," he interrupted her. "Who gave you the money to buy the food and clothes? Who offered you his name and all that goes with it when you told me you were pregnant?"

She opened her mouth and Bieito poked her in the arm. Esperanza shifted away, glaring at him.

"You were the one who turned me down and told me you wanted nothing to do with my life. I did everything I could to make sure you and Kemen were taken care of while abiding by the oath you made me take." Victor clasped his hands behind his back. "This is not my fault, Esperanza. You were the one who broke your word, telling your boyfriend about our son."

"I was lonely," she whined.

Quirking an eyebrow at her, he chuckled. "You've had lovers since shortly after you had Kemen. There was no way you were lonely. I'm not an idiot."

Bieito coughed, drawing Victor's attention to him. He tilted his wrist, showing Victor his watch, and Victor realized they were going to have to get moving if they were going to leave by six. Nodding, he dropped his gaze back to Esperanza, trying to figure out what to do with her.

"Valdez brought me the license plate number from the car Señora Larenz drove here," Bieito spoke up.

"Yes?" He didn't take his focus off her and he saw her cringe. "What did you do, Esperanza?"

"It's registered to the Mederiz Corporation."

He stiffened. "Really?"

"I double-checked, sir." Bieito didn't sound happy and Victor knew why.

"So, it seems to me you might have known more about this whole situation than you said." Crouching down, he took her chin in his hand again and forced her to meet his gaze. "Why are you driving a car registered to a dummy corporation owned by the Cortez cartel?"

She tried to shake her head. "I don't know who owns the car. It's the one Mitch uses when he's home."

He inhaled deeply then let it out loudly. "Oh, I do believe you think I'm stupid, but at the moment, I don't have time to deal with you. We're going to the city to rescue my son. You'll be kept here, locked in your suite."

"You can't do that," she protested.

"I can't? Really? You have no idea exactly what I can do. I can't have you calling Cortez—or anyone—about what we're doing. The men I leave to watch you will take your phone. You will get fed. I'm not a monster, Esperanza. Once we get Kemen back, I'll be back to take care of you."

He could see she wanted to argue with him. Tightening his grip, he growled at her and her eyes went wide as she paled. "No! Don't say a word. You don't get to tell me how much you love Kemen when you helped put him in the position he's in right now. If you had kept your mouth shut, he would be out with his friends or at home asleep. He wouldn't be in the hands of my worst enemy."

"Sir." Bieito's soft voice broke into the anger welling inside him.

After letting her go, he stood. "Have Rodriguez escort her to her suite and make sure he takes any items she might have brought with her, especially her phone. I'm going upstairs to change. We'll leave in a half hour."

"Yes, sir." Bieito lifted Esperanza to her feet then dragged her from the study.

Victor could hear her yelling for him, but he wasn't interested in her any more. At one time, she'd been a fond memory of his college days. He liked remembering the time they'd spent together, and the fact that she was the mother of his only child had kept him from cutting all ties to her.

To find out she'd betrayed him in the deepest way possible—by using his son to help his enemies—caused his hands to tremble with the force of his anger. He stalked over to the fireplace and looked up at the portrait of his mother.

"How could a mother do that to her child? You hated what Father had become, but you chose to leave instead of risking Pablo's life," he muttered. "I'm many things, Mama, yet even I wouldn't use my son in such a way."

There was no answer to be given. Suddenly, Victor wanted to hear Pablo's voice to know his brother was safe. He couldn't call. Not only was it too late at night, he had to cut ties with Pablo for a while to ensure the American law enforcement didn't catch on to their relationship.

"Now, we must go upstairs and change. Valdez has the men and the weapons ready to go. As soon as we are dressed, we can leave," Bieito told him.

"Bieito, what am I going to do? How do I make this up to my son?" He shoved his hands through his hair.

"First, you rescue him. Then by kill the men who dared to put their hands on him. After that, it's up to him how he'll handle the news about his mother and whether or not he wants to have anything to do with you." Bieito touched his shoulder. "Come. We must go."

Victor let Bieito direct him from the study then up the stairs. As he changed, he grabbed a hold of his emotions and shoved them behind an impenetrable wall. All of what he was feeling would have to wait. Kemen didn't need the guilt-ridden father coming to his rescue. He needed the vicious drug lord who never let anyone stop him from getting what he wanted. And what he wanted was his son.

Chapter Six

Their driver brought the SUV to a stop in front of the large, wrought-iron gate then rolled down the window to punch in the access code. Bieito shook Victor slightly.

"Sir, we're here," he murmured as the gate started to swing open.

Victor woke instantly. Bieito had never seen Victor sleepy—or even half asleep—since they started sharing a bed during the night. No matter how quietly he tried to leave and return to his own room, he'd always turn around at the door to see Victor watching him go. He wouldn't admit how much he'd love for Victor to stop him then ask him to stay the whole night. Bieito wasn't sure if it would ever happen.

"Once we're inside, you call Pablo while I make sure Jorge is waiting for us. I can talk to him alone if you wish," he suggested, but Victor shook his head.

"No. I want to be there when he tells you his information. Also, we need to arrange to get the money delivered for the ransom payment." Victor's dark eyes were hard. He seemed to have buried any emotion he might have been feeling since Esperanza's appearance at the compound.

The façade of the cold, calculating drug lord had returned, and while Bieito hated to see the true Victor disappear underneath it, he understood why it had to be. The news about Kemen being his son might have gotten out to the public, but that didn't mean Victor could show any feelings toward the young man. He had to remain unmoved and uncaring, or else Kemen could be faced with worse torture than he was probably enduring at the moment.

"Yes, sir. I'll determine whether Jorge is here or not before I begin to go through our accounts to find the cash." Bieito turned his face to the window, grimacing at the thought of having to liquidate some of the stock Victor owned. Luckily, he wouldn't have to do much, considering they kept a lot of cash on hand for shipments and other activities.

Drug trafficking was really a mostly cash business, as were the various other criminal enterprises the cartel indulged in. Bieito had been the one to diversify Victor's wealth, putting it into accounts throughout the country and internationally. He'd done it in such a way that he didn't have to trust anyone else with the money.

He made sure not to mingle the cartel income with any of Victor's legit businesses—or any of his own either. The way he had it set up, if the federal agencies ever arrested them and tried to freeze their assets, they wouldn't get every last penny they had.

Bieito had seen too many who worked for the cartels getting arrested, and while he understood there was a price to pay for what they were doing, he wasn't going to let them take it all. Not that it really mattered. He didn't have anyone to leave his wealth to, and there was no way he would be getting out of jail if the Americans had their way.

Shaking off the thought, he refocused on his surroundings. He climbed out of the back once the vehicle had stopped in front of the house then walked around to join Victor. Their group of ten guards surrounded them before ushering them inside. Bieito didn't look around, not wanting to give anyone who might be watching satisfaction by acting nervous.

Once inside, Bieito turned to find Romero, the man in charge of the house when Victor wasn't in residence.

"Is Jorge here?"

Romero shook his head. "He's about five minutes away, boss. He was waiting for one last bit of information to come in before he left."

Bieito nodded then glanced over to Victor. "Why don't you go make the call you need to take care of? I'll bring him in when he gets here."

Victor didn't reply, just continued farther into the house. Bieito wasn't insulted by being ignored since it wasn't often Victor chose to acknowledge him when they were surrounded by the men.

After he disappeared, Bieito gestured for Valdez and Romero to walk with him. "I need you both to make sure the guards are on alert while we're here. Romero, tell me, has there been any news about a kidnapping of a young university student?"

Romero narrowed his eyes while he thought then he shook his head. "I haven't heard anything, sir, but I can check and see."

"Yes. Do that and bring me whatever you discover, and make sure you bring Jorge to me as soon as he arrives." He dismissed Romero before meeting Valdez's gaze. "You have an idea of who the student is. I wish to remind you that staying quiet about your suspicions can only help to prolong your life. In addition, you might find yourself with a bonus in your pay later."

"Yes, sir." Valdez didn't show any emotion at the idea of extra money. Of course, he knew his life would be forfeited if he gossiped about any of his thoughts. Bieito didn't have to remind him about that.

"Now go and check on the security. I want a report in twenty minutes," he said before stalking to the study where he knew he'd find Victor.

Victor was just setting his phone down onto the desk when Bieito entered. "Is everything all right with Pablo?" he asked softly, even though there was no one else in the room with them.

"Yes. I didn't tell him about what was going on down here. He was happy to know we were fine and asked that I try harder to stay in touch. Also, he said Ken is recovering from his injuries." Victor seemed to be distracted by something.

Bieito frowned. "What injuries? I guess I didn't know he'd been hurt."

Looking at him, Victor grimaced. "Apparently, he'd been working with the DEA to intercept shipments of drugs and illegals at the border. It wasn't just one of the cartels they targeted. Unfortunately, the cartels discovered—or thought they knew—he'd been ratting them out, and they tortured him to tell which agent he was helping."

He winced, knowing exactly what would have happened to Ken during the time the cartel had him. Bieito knew because he'd done the same to snitches. "I'm glad to hear he's doing well. How did they find him though? I would've thought the cartel would've hidden him far better than that."

"DEA had help finding him, from what I understand." Victor seemed to shake off whatever was bothering him. "Has Jorge arrived yet?"

"No, sir. One of his men had information that he wanted to get before he came here. I'm sure he's scared to death that he won't have all the important details and I'll kill him where he stands." Bieito snorted.

"You've done a very good job of ensuring all the men know not to cross you. We've made sure to instill the fear of God into them," Victor replied.

They had and Bieito didn't regret one minute of it since, ultimately, it was to keep Victor safe. If any of the men at any time thought Victor was weak, they'd go for him like sharks in a feeding frenzy. He couldn't allow that to happen. His life wasn't just working for the Delarosa family. It was Victor himself.

Victor shifted, drawing Bieito's attention back to the present, and he cleared his throat. "I'm going to have to start gathering the money."

"We have enough, right?" Victor removed his suit coat then tossed it over the back of the leather couch placed near one wall. He unbuttoned his cuffs before rolling up his sleeves.

"Yes. I'll need all of those three days to get it, but we do have it. It'll come from the cartel's accounts. I'm not going to touch your personal money." He removed his jacket as well, adjusting the shoulder holster under his left arm afterward. Running his hand through his hair, he organized his plans in his mind.

Waving in a dismissive gesture, Victor wandered over to the side bar before pouring out two highballs of whiskey. He brought one to Bieito. "Here, have a drink."

"It's only ten," he pointed out but took a sip anyway.

"Who the fuck cares what time it is? It's been a very long night and day so far. I'm not saying drink the whole bottle, but one glass will help take us away from the edge we've been balancing on since Esperanza showed up on our doorstep." Victor touched Bieito's hand for a second.

A knock sounded on the door and Bieito stepped farther away, schooling his expression back to its normal iciness. Victor told them to come in. Romero entered first, followed by Jorge, who stopped a few feet inside the room then bowed slightly.

"Señor Delarosa. Señor Perez."

"Come in and sit, Jorge. We need to know everything you've found out about Kemen Larenz and what happened yesterday." Victor gestured to the chairs in front of his desk. "Romero, can you have a maid bring us some coffee and breakfast? We didn't eat before we left the compound."

"Yes, sir." Romero inclined his head then left.

After Jorge sat, Victor took his place behind the desk while Bieito propped his hip against the edge of it. He motioned for Jorge to begin.

"Tell us," he ordered.

He watched as Jorge pulled some papers from his inner pocket and looked them over before talking. Hearing Victor huff a breath of annoyance behind him made him want to smile, but he kept his face blank. Bieito put his hand on the desk then tapped the surface with it as a signal to Victor to rein in his exasperation. Pushing Jorge was going to get him flustered and he'd take longer to tell them.

Bieito had figured that out while dealing with the man. Jorge was good being in charge of their operations in Mexico City and the men who handed the shipments for them. Yet he wasn't good at talking face-to-face with his bosses, and Bieito was pretty sure Jorge was ready to piss himself if Victor so much as glared at him.

"Take your time, Jorge. We need to make sure the information is correct before we can do anything about it." While he wasn't in the mood to be encouraging, he understood it was better than threatening him.

"I got it." Jorge cleared his throat. "The kid was taken from a café downtown. I can give you the name and everything."

"Not important," Bieito informed him. "Go on."

He heard Victor inhale behind him, and he shook his head to keep him from saying anything.

"Larenz was having breakfast with some friends when a black Ford truck pulled up in the street and four men jumped out. Three of them were armed with AK-47s. The fourth had a 9mm that he pointed at the young man and then ordered him to get in the truck." As he read from the paper, Jorge relaxed. He let the sheets drop to his lap before looking up at Bieito.

"Has anyone talked to the friends? Got their statements?"

Jorge nodded. "Yes, boss, but they hadn't returned by the time I left. I told them to come directly here when they were done."

"That's fine. We'll get back to them later." Victor spoke up and Jorge jerked at his harsh voice. "Go on with your report."

Jorge swallowed loudly enough for Bieito to hear him. "Larenz fought with them until he was hit on the head and dazed. The four men dragged him into the truck and drove off." He shuffled through the papers then nodded when he found what he was looking for. "My men were able to figure out that the truck drove almost straight to Cortez's main warehouse here in the city. Unfortunately, they were unable to find out if the kid remains there now or not, though as far as could be determined, he might have been moved last night. But I don't know where yet."

Straightening, Bieito held out his hand. "Give me those. Why don't you go out and get something to drink from Romero? Don't go anywhere. When your men show up, bring them here. I'm sure Señor Delarosa will have other things to ask you."

"All right, boss." Jorge stood then bowed to Victor. "Señor Delarosa."

Waiting until Jorge had shut the door behind him, Bieito handed the papers to Victor. "I guess my first order of business is to head to the warehouse and see whether Kemen is still there or not."

Victor nodded, his gaze on the report in front of him, but Bieito could tell he wasn't seeing it. "Yes, go and do that, though my gut is telling me they moved him last night before we were informed of him being taken."

He agreed. "Yes, but we need to make sure. I'll also get the process of following their trail started. At least we know for certain that it was Cortez who took him."

"Was there really any doubt?" Victor slammed his fist onto the desk. "I should've kept Esperanza from seeing Manchester. I knew the man was an addict and couldn't be trusted."

"How would you have done that? Killed him? Imprisoned her?"

Victor shot him a cold glance and Bieito chuckled.

"No, you wouldn't have done either of those. You could've cut off her income, I guess, but since she seems to believe they're in love, it might not have worked."

He saw the guilt hidden in Victor's eyes. After walking around the desk, he crouched next to him then rested his hands on Victor's thighs. "I'm afraid, aside from telling me, there was no way you could stop this from happening. If it wasn't Cortez, it would've been one of your other enemies, Victor. I know it's hard to hear when you're the god of your world, but it's true. You're only human and can only do so much."

"I should've told you earlier, then you could've ensured this wouldn't happen," Victor muttered.

"You might be right. Then again, it could've happened even with the guards he would've had. No one is infallible, not even God. Mistakes have been made. We'll do our best to fix them. First, we must find where they've taken Kemen, then we'll go after him." He squeezed Victor's legs before pushing to his feet. "I'm going to go talk to the banks and get the ball rolling on the money. Then I'll take a couple of men and go nose around the warehouse."

Victor frowned then said, "Be careful if you're going during the day. I don't want you getting shot. You're too important."

He wasn't sure how important he really was, though he was the only one who could keep Victor from completely losing it and killing every person who was pissing him off. *Well*, he amended. *Victor wouldn't go that crazy.*

Bieito shot a quick glance over his shoulder then bent to brush a fast kiss over Victor's lips. Usually, he wouldn't take a liberty like that, but he had a feeling Victor needed to be reassured, which freaked him out slightly. Victor Delarosa should never be less than arrogant and sure of his place as the center of the universe.

Victor squinted at him. "Why?"

"Just felt like it. If Jorge's men get here before I leave for the warehouse, I'll have them brought in to see you." He waited for Victor's dismissal.

"Fine. I need to read this then go over some of the reports Romero's piled up on my desk while I was gone." Victor gestured to a few files Bieito had spotted when he'd walked in earlier.

"Sir." Bieito inclined his head then left.

Chapter Seven

Snap ended the call then set his phone on the table. Staring at Ken, he pursed his lips. *Do I tell him about this, or do I continue ignoring the connection he has with Delarosa?* He rubbed his hand over his bald head in frustration. *How the hell does Mac do this?*

"Who was that?" Ken stood in front of the stove and glanced at him over his shoulder. "Do you have to go in to the office?"

"What?" He shook his head. "No. Dalton just wanted to give me a heads-up about a situation in Mexico."

Because he was watching Ken closely, he saw the stiffness in his lover's shoulders. After standing, he strolled over to him then encircled his waist to pull Ken back against his chest. He nuzzled Ken's neck, and Ken sighed, relaxing into him.

"Does it have to do with Delarosa?" Ken's question was soft.

Sighing, Snap nodded. "Yeah. Seems there's a dispute happening between Delarosa and the Cortez cartel. No one is entirely sure what's going on, just that there is a situation brewing. One of the warehouses that the Mexican drug task force has under surveillance has been seeing a lot of activity lately. It's a suspected Cortez holding center. Plus Delarosa is said to be in the city, which is weird since he rarely goes to Mexico City, preferring to stay out in the rural area on one of his compounds."

"Okay. Are the Mexicans going to try to arrest him if they think he's in town?" Ken finished cooking their supper and Snap stepped back to allow him to dish them out. Then he took the full plates while Ken grabbed the salad. "Is that why Dalton called? Are you going to have to go down there?"

He set the food down before motioning for Ken to sit. "Not yet. They're still trying to figure out exactly what is going on between Cortez and Delarosa. There was a university student kidnapped yesterday at gunpoint from one of the Mexican cafés. The police are saying that it was Cortez' men who took him. They don't know whether that's related or not yet."

Ken picked up his fork then returned it to the table. He met Snap's gaze with his own troubled one. "How am I supposed to feel about this? I know Tanner is probably going out of his mind with worry, but I've never met Victor. I know nothing about him except he's a drug lord, and those kinds of people are evil."

Snap couldn't argue with that. He knew some of the things Delarosa had been accused of doing, and he didn't doubt that a majority of them were true. Yet he knew Tanner and Mac. Both were good men, so there had to be something inside Delarosa—buried deep under the monster—that had convinced them he was redeemable in some way.

"I don't know, Ken. All I know is you have the right to feel however you want to feel. Tanner doesn't expect you to love Delarosa like he does. He's happy having you around to hang out with, especially since we won't be seeing Delarosa back here any time soon."

Ken held out his hand and Snap took it. "I like having Tanner as a brother. I tend to forget we're any relation to Delarosa."

"That's a good thing." He gestured to his plate. "Now let's eat, because I have plans for you after supper."

"Oh, you do, huh?" Ken's face lit up.

Snap nodded. "Yes, and you're going to need all the energy you can get for it."

Ken's laughter lifted the worry from Snap's mind. There wasn't anything he could do about the cartels at that exact moment. He'd enjoy the night with his lover. He'd come so close to losing Ken, he didn't want to miss out any more time together.

* * * *

"Come in," Victor called from where he sat at his desk. He watched as Bieito strolled into his office.

He barely kept from licking his lips at the sight of his tall, handsome lover dressed all in black. Bieito had been busy all day, working on getting the money for the ransom, that he hadn't been able to go out and check the warehouse until after the sun set. Now he and four of his most trusted men were leaving. He wore a tight, black, long-sleeved shirt, black cargo pants and combat boots. A knife was sheathed on his right thigh while a 9mm was holstered on his left.

Bieito looked dangerous and Victor found himself fighting the sudden urge to bend the man over his desk and fuck him until he screamed Victor's name as he came. He trailed his gaze from the tips of Bieito's boots to the top of the black ball cap he wore. Victor let his eyes linger on the telltale bulge behind Bieito's zipper. Someone else was just as excited as he was.

"We're getting ready to leave," Bieito informed him, coming to stand in the middle of the room. He clasped his hands behind his back as he met Victor's gaze. "Valdez and Romero have security here while I'm gone."

"Good." Victor stood then stalked around the corner of his desk into Bieito's personal space. After reaching up, he grabbed Bieito's head to jerk him down into a crushing kiss. He took what he wanted and there wasn't any resistance. Bieito never fought him. He always gave anything—and everything—to Victor.

When his lungs burned for air, he stepped back, but not before biting Bieito's bottom lip. They stood there, panting and staring at each other for a minute until they heard movement in the hallway. Victor eased farther back in case someone came in.

"Be careful," he ordered his lover.

"Always, sir." Bieito's intense gaze met his. "Do you want me to report to you when we return?"

Victor inhaled then exhaled slowly. That would give Bieito the perfect reason to come to Victor's room and they could fuck then. "Yes. I want to know the minute you arrive back."

Bieito bowed slightly. "Certainly, sir."

He strolled over to the side bar to pour a drink, not wanting to watch Bieito leave. Intellectually, he knew Bieito was more than capable of protecting himself. Hell, the man was a trained killer, for Christ's sake. Yet Victor couldn't help but wish he didn't have to send Bieito out on jobs like the one he was going on.

Men would die tonight, more than likely at Bieito's hands.

Victor wanted to slap himself upside the head for worrying about Bieito and the damage he'd done to the man's soul. The thing he needed to remember was Bieito could've left the business at any point in time, especially while he was going to school in Berkeley, but he hadn't. After completing his degree in record time, he'd come back to Mexico and the Delarosa cartel.

His return had caught Victor's attention then Bieito had captured his interest. It wasn't long before they were fucking, and Victor was sure people would be surprised to find out that Bieito had been the aggressor at first. He'd been reluctant to initiate any kind of relationship with the younger Perez, not wanting Bieito to feel like he had to sleep with the boss, even though he'd found Bieito quite gorgeous.

He'd known he liked both sexes since he was a teenager, but had never given voice to the attraction to men because he knew his father would have beaten the shit out of him. Victor gave a soft snort. His father had to be rolling in his grave now, considering all three of his sons were in relationships with men, though Victor knew he was the only one his father would've cared about.

His thoughts wandered back to Bieito. The first time they'd fucked, Victor had fought against allowing any deeper feelings to develop for Bieito. He'd wanted to convince himself that it was just a convenient opportunity—that it was easier to fuck Bieito then find someone else to share his bed. At least he knew Bieito wouldn't try to blackmail him. The man had as much to lose as Victor had. Then once their fathers had died, they'd been able to relax a little, though not enough to chance getting caught by anyone.

Settling behind his desk, he decided to go through some of the files he hadn't wanted Bieito to see. He placed his glass down then reached for the first report. By the time he got through all of them, he had a list and determined it was time to make a phone call.

* * * *

The squeak of the door opening woke Victor later in the night. He lay in the darkness, straining to hear any other noise that would alert him to who—and where—the intruder might be. He slid his hand under his pillow, wrapping his fingers around the grip of his 9mm. As he drew it out, he slid the safety off while trying to determine where the person was.

"If you shoot me now, you won't get fucked tonight," Bieito spoke from the shadows.

"Bastard." Victor snarled, making sure the safety was back on before he set the gun on the nightstand. Reaching over, he turned the lamp on then swore when he saw Bieito. "What the fuck happened?"

Bieito finished stripping off his shirt then let it fall to the floor. He shook his head when Victor began to climb out of bed. "Don't. I'm going to take a shower and clean up. When I get back, I'll tell you what happened."

"Are you all right?" It was the only thing that mattered right then for Victor.

"Yes. I'm fine. I had the doctor stitch up the cuts."

He leaped from under the covers to grab Bieito by the hand and drag him closer to the light. "Where are these cuts? How did you get them? You can't take a shower without getting the stitches wet."

Bieito sighed, letting Victor turn him in every direction to check him over. He didn't protest when Victor pushed him toward the bathroom.

"We'll wash you off, but no soaking them," he said as he motioned for Bieito to finish taking off his clothes. He turned the faucet on in the sink before digging out some washcloths and soap. "Explain how all of this happened."

"It was my fault. Had my mind on other things when we got there. I should've known Cortez would have more guards than we saw patrolling the warehouse. We got all the way inside without encountering too much resistance. Should've been my first clue that something wasn't right." Bieito shook his head. "They jumped us as we were crossing the floor of the warehouse to get to the stairs leading to the second level."

Victor wet the cloth then wiped at Bieito's chin. "That's not like you. What were you thinking about so intensely that you forgot where you were?"

Bieito's gaze swept around the room and Victor could tell he didn't want to meet Victor's eyes. *It has to do with Kemen, Esperanza and me. He's wondering where he stands because I never told him about my son.*

Grabbing a hold of Bieito's chin, he forced it around so they were face-to-face. Those dark eyes held uncertainty — an emotion Victor never thought he'd seen Bieito experience before. Realizing that he'd put it there caused his chest to tighten.

"I really was going to tell you last night before Esperanza arrived," he informed him. When Bieito tried to shift his gaze, Victor shook his chin slightly. "I mean it. It was time for you to know. Maybe I had a feeling something like this would happen. If anyone could've kept Kemen safe for me, it would've been you. There's no one else I trust to protect those I love."

Bieito licked his lips. Ignoring the smears of blood and dirt, Victor leaned in to press his mouth to Bieito's. He demanded entrance and Bieito opened, allowing him to sweep his tongue inside. Victor threaded his fingers into the curls at the back of Bieito's head and held him tightly so he couldn't move away. Not that he would ever try to get away from Victor. No, Bieito was completely Victor's and he'd try to never take advantage of that.

Yet I have used his love to get him to do things for me. Guilt hit him hard, but he couldn't take back what he'd done. All he could was hope Bieito didn't decide to leave after the situation had been dealt with. There were only so many insults a man could take to his pride, and Victor knew he might have pushed Bieito too far with Kemen and Esperanza.

He claimed Bieito as best he could right there, nipping Bieito's lip then sucking to ease the pain. He rubbed his thumb over his lover's cheek. "It's Kemen I love, not Esperanza. The moment she told me she didn't want to marry me but was willing to take my money instead, we were done. I was willing to pay her to keep my son safe."

Bieito snorted and Victor rolled his eyes.

"I know. She did a good job until this druggie got to her. I should've gotten you to scare him away from her. It was too late by the time I made the decision to tell you. I just didn't know that."

He went back to washing the mess from Bieito's skin, taking care around the knife wounds. It didn't surprise Victor when Bieito didn't make a sound, not even when Victor had to scrub at some of the spots to get them clean. His lover had never been a man to complain or whine about his life. Bieito marched straight ahead, expecting everyone—except Victor—to move out of his way.

"All right. We're done." Victor rinsed out the cloth then drained the sink. "Was Kemen there?"

"No." Bieito frowned. "After we got rid of the guards, we searched the warehouse high and low. If he was there, they moved him quickly instead of risking you coming in and rescuing him."

"Did you find anything else there?" He took a hold of Bieito's hand, leading him back into the bedroom.

"There were a lot of bales of marijuana. I think they're getting ready to send a major shipment out." Bieito dropped to the edge of the mattress and let his hands hang between his knees. "There's a room where they were packaging cocaine and heroin for transport as well. I'm rather amazed the police haven't raided them yet."

Victor hummed under his breath. "Something tells me it won't be long before they do."

He shoved Bieito until he lay back against the pillows then crawled over to straddle his waist. Bieito rested his hands on Victor's hips, staring up at him. Smiling, Victor ground their groins together and Bieito moaned.

"I'll be careful," Victor promised. "But you have to tell me if I hurt you. No being a tough guy."

Bieito nodded then swallowed. "Yes, sir."

He chuckled. "That's right. I'm your boss and you need to listen to my orders."

Making sure he didn't put pressure anywhere else, Victor rocked against Bieito, loving how amazing it felt when he rubbed their erections together. Hot, soft skin over rock hard flesh. He imagined he could probably get both of them off just doing that, but he wanted Bieito inside him. Hell, he needed Bieito to claim him in the most primitive way possible.

"Do you want me to get you ready?" Bieito asked, as he smoothed his hands up and down Victor's sides.

"No. I'll be fine. We'll take it slow." He reached behind him to take Bieito's cock in hand. Biting his bottom lip, he slowly lowered himself, trying not to tense when the flared head breached his hole.

By the time he was fully seated on Bieito, both of them were covered in sweat and Victor was trembling. He exhaled the breath he'd been holding then leaned forward to brush a kiss over Bieito's mouth.

When he eased away, Bieito tightened his hold on his hips and said, "You should've let me stretch you or at least used lube. You don't have to punish yourself for this stupid situation."

"I'm not doing that." He paused as he thought about it. "Not entirely. I like the burn. You know that."

Bieito nodded, obviously wanting to say something else, but Victor didn't want to hear it. Not right then. Rising up on his knees, he let Bieito slide almost all the way out before he impaled himself again. He kept the tempo slow and easy as he did his best to build Bieito's need without hurting him.

He gasped when Bieito placed his feet on the mattress then lifted his hips to meet each of Victor's downward strokes. The angle changed, causing Bieito to nail Victor's gland every time, and he could feel pressure behind his balls.

"Touch me," he demanded.

"Yes, sir." Bieito winked as he wrapped his large hand around Victor's shaft then pumped in time with their fucking.

Just what he needed. He threw back his head and cried out as he came, spilling his cum over Bieito's fingers and stomach. A few more thrusts and Bieito grunted, flooding Victor's ass. Victor did his best to massage every last drop from Bieito until he could no longer hold himself upright.

Flopping over onto his side, he winced as Bieito slipped from him then grimaced at the rush of cum over his thighs. Bieito started to climb out of the bed, but Victor placed his hand on his chest.

"Where do you think you're going?"

"I was going to get something to clean you up with," Bieito said.

He shook his head. "No. As soon as I can move, I'll go take care of it. You need to rest."

Bieito must have been hurting since he didn't argue, he just settled back under the covers. Victor got up, took care of everything and by the time he returned, Bieito was asleep. Brushing some hair back from Bieito's forehead, Victor pressed a kiss to his temple.

"Sleep well," he whispered before digging a phone out of his nightstand. He had to make a call then he'd join Bieito, and hopefully, they'd both get some rest by the morning.

Chapter Eight

"You were right," Bieito said as he walked into Victor's office the next morning.

"About what?" Victor didn't look up from the file he studied.

Bieito set one of the cups of coffee he'd been carrying next to Victor's elbow before taking his customary seat. "About Cortez's warehouse being raided soon. I got confirmation that the army and the American DEA went in early this morning."

Victor grunted before taking a sip. Once that was done, he met Bieito's gaze. "Tell me what we're doing to find Kemen."

He put his own cup on the corner of the desk then tugged out his tablet. "I have Jorge out with his men, scouring the city, but I have a feeling they've taken him somewhere outside the capital."

"North or south?" Victor tapped his fingers on the pile of papers covering most of the surface in front of him.

Bieito wrinkled his nose as he considered both options. "Wisdom would say they'd take him south into the territory they control."

Victor shook his head. "Fuck wisdom. What does your gut tell you?"

"They took him north into the States. While Jorge is out in the city, I've got guys I can trust looking in both directions. They only know they're looking for Kemen, not why we want him. I actually told them Kemen made off with a lot of your money, then fell into Cortez' hands."

He waited to see if Victor was going to tell him to change the story, but Victor didn't seem inclined to do so.

"They think you want him back to teach him a lesson. I told them if they find him to let me know. You want to deal with Cortez and Kemen on your own." He scrolled through the names on his tablet. "I talked to Romero, and he said Señora Larenz is throwing a tantrum. She tried to hurt one of the maids earlier."

Victor snarled. "I'll call Romero. She won't treat my employees like that."

Bieito hid his little shudder at the sound of Victor's annoyance. He'd experienced very few moments when Victor had been angry with him, and those times were more than enough for him to do everything he could not to have it happen again.

"I told him to expect a call from you at some point today. We have four shipments crossing the border at three different ports of entry. More than likely, two of them will get through." He'd worked out the odds every time he sent curriers out. If two out of four made it across then he figured they were still doing well.

"Let me know how those turn out, though you should put someone in charge of that since you'll be traveling with me to get Kemen." Victor whirled around in his chair to stare through the large window while he sipped at his coffee.

He waited Victor out. There was no point in pushing the man when there wasn't a rush right then. Bieito sent a text to Jorge to find out what was going on with him. The silence filled the room for a few minutes, so Bieito began to work on arranging how to get the money he was gathering to the house.

"How is the ransom coming?" Victor spoke.

"I've got it all settled and just confirmed the last hundred thousand. I've got runners bringing it here so we can organize it. When—or if—they call, you can tell them the ransom will be ready on the deadline." Bieito couldn't help but smile. He'd done the impossible, and he was pretty sure the Cortez cartel hadn't expected him to get the money together in time. He caught the look Victor shot him from over his shoulder and nodded.

"Impressive. I guess I didn't realize we had access to that much cash so quickly." Victor shrugged. "It's a good thing you're loyal to me or you could probably embezzle a lot of my money without me noticing."

Bieito snorted. "Right. You know every cent in every account I've set up for you. I'm sure you had no doubt I could pull it together."

The phone rang before Victor answered, so Bieito answered it. "Hello."

"I want to talk to Delarosa," the gruff voice replied.

"What is this in regards to?" he asked, though he had a feeling he knew what it was about.

"He'll know. Just give him the damn phone."

Bieito held out the receiver to Victor. "It's for you."

Victor took it and bared his teeth. "I've been waiting for your call. I don't have all day to waste while you get your nuts off by jerking me around. What do you want now?"

He bit back his smile when Victor rolled his eyes at whatever the man said.

"Yes, I have the money. I don't need the third day, so can we just get on with this whole ransom thing?" Victor curled his lip. "I told you before, but it bears repeating. When I find you, I'll gut you like a fish and spit on you while you bleed to death. No one gets away with extorting money from me. Also, pass on this message to your puppet master, Cortez. Death is coming for him on swift and sure wings. He's signed his death warrant by coming after me."

Another moment of silence then Victor grunted before slamming the phone down. Bieito kept his mouth shut while Victor swore loudly and creatively. After walking over to the side bar, Bieito picked up a decanter of whiskey, holding it so Victor could see it. He poured out a high ball full when Victor nodded.

"Some might say it's too early in the morning for this, but I think the day you've had so far, you deserve it." He handed it over and watched as Victor drank it down. "Do you want more?"

Victor shook his head. "No matter how I downplay what Kemen means to me, they know he's my son and are assuming I'll do anything to get him back."

"They aren't wrong," Bieito pointed out, studying Victor.

Setting the empty glass on the desk, Victor said, "They're right. I will give my entire fortune to get him back, though I know they aren't planning to return Kemen alive. If we don't find him before they get their money, Cortez will kill him and all I'll get back is his body."

"That won't happen." Bieito rested his hand on Victor's shoulder. "You know I won't let them kill Kemen. If he's still alive, we'll find and rescue him."

Shock rushed through him when Victor swung around to snuggle close. He closed his arms around Victor's shoulders, holding him tight. Bieito rested his cheek on the top of Victor's head.

"You'll do your best, Bieito, and that's all I can ask of you, but you aren't Superman. Neither are the men who work for us." Victor sounded resigned to whatever happened to Kemen. "I must accept whatever happens, whether he lives or dies."

"He won't die." Maybe he shouldn't promise that, but he'd never seen Victor like this.

There was a knock on the door, and they broke apart. Victor took his seat again while Bieito moved to the other window but kept his back to it.

"Come in," Victor yelled.

Valdez pushed open the door then stepped into the room. "Señor Delarosa. Boss." He bowed to both of them.

"Yes, Valdez?" Victor motioned for him to come closer.

"I wasn't sure if Jorge had gotten back with you yet, sir." Valdez looked at Bieito.

Bieito double-checked his phone then shook his head. "Not yet. Why?"

"One of my men informed me that he knows someone who's part of the Cortez cartel. I told him to grab him and bring him here. He might be able to tell us where they've taken the man you're looking for." Valdez looked a little nervous, as though he wasn't sure if Victor would praise him or yell at him.

Bieito thought it showed initiative to do that, and he wasn't going to bust Valdez's balls for it. He wasn't so sure how Victor felt though.

"Good job. When they get here, come get Bieito and he'll question the man." Victor raised an eyebrow when Valdez didn't leave. "Was there anything else?"

Valdez frowned then said, "How did you want me to handle the fact my guy knows one of Cortez's men?"

Bieito had to admit it was a good question. He moved closer to the desk before propping his hip against it. Valdez swallowed but didn't step back. Bieito gave him credit, considering Bieito was taller and outweighed him by several pounds. Also, there had been more than once where Bieito had disciplined Valdez for different infractions.

Victor snorted. "We all know people who work for Cortez. Hell, I know the bastard himself. As long as you're sure he's loyal to us and not giving Cortez information, I don't see why we need to do anything to him."

"I'm sure of him. He wasn't happy about admitting to know the other guy. I think there's bad blood between them or something." Valdez shrugged. "I'll keep an eye on him though, just in case he's pulling a fast one on me."

"Good." Bieito straightened. "Either come and get me or text me. I'll join you in the shed."

"Yes, boss." Valdez bowed to Victor then Bieito before he left.

"I need to make sure the money is in transit and check on some other issues while we wait." He checked with Victor, who merely nodded at him. "I'll see you at lunch then."

Victor waved him out and he headed to his own office just down the hall. He settled in to do the other work he was responsible for while also starting to organize what he thought they might need to rescue Kemen.

* * * *

Tanner grabbed the phone as it rang. He glanced at the number and frowned. It wasn't one he recognized, but he answered anyway.

"Hello?" He got up to shut the door of his office at the teen center.

"Pablo?"

His heart skipped a beat when Victor's voice came through. "Victor? Are you all right?"

His brother chuckled. "I'm fine, *hermano*. How are you and your Ranger getting along?"

"We're doing well," he said as he dropped back into his chair. "Is Perez all right as well?"

"He's fine. We're dealing with a situation right now, but it should be taken care of in the next couple of days." Victor paused for a few seconds then asked, "How are Kenneth and Jefferson? Has he recovered fully from his injuries?"

Tanner was a little surprised that Victor acknowledged their half-brother, but he wasn't going to say anything. "He's doing well. The doctors say he'll always limp, and he lost two fingers on his right hand."

Grunting, Victor then said, "I'm sorry. I'm sure Jefferson is supporting him while he has to deal with this. At least I hope he is."

"Oh yes. Snap has been taking good care of Ken." He rubbed his forehead. "I'm glad you called. I was worried you might be in trouble after going back down there."

"I only wanted to check in. I might not be in touch for a while. Perez and I must deal with the problem here, so I won't be able to call you." Victor sounded distracted.

Tanner didn't usually second-guess Victor, but there was something making Tanner uncomfortable about their conversation. "Are you sure you're both okay?"

Victor sighed. "Yes, Pablo. I'm sure. It's been a long couple of days and I haven't slept well. I need to be going, but as soon as I can, I'll call you to see how things are."

"Be careful. I trust Perez to keep you safe. Just don't do anything that will cause him to break his promise to me," Tanner ordered Victor.

"His promise to you?"

"I made Perez promise he wouldn't let you get hurt. You have so many enemies, not just the other cartels, but the governments as well. I know you'll end paying for your crimes eventually, but I'm hoping it won't end with you dying. I like having both my brothers alive, even if I can't spend any time with one of them." His heart ached with the knowledge of all the years they'd missed making memories like brothers should.

Victor hummed softly before he said, "Our family seems to have abused Perez's willing nature for many years. We'll keep each other safe, Pablo. I'm not going to let anything happen to Perez either."

The statement didn't surprise Tanner. He'd guessed several years ago there was something more going on between Victor and Perez than just Perez being Victor's right-hand man. Yet the people who populated their world frowned upon their kind of relationship. He'd always hoped there was a way for

Victor and Perez to live and love openly, but it was impossible as long as they continued on the path they'd taken.

"I have to go now. If I'm able, I'll call you, but try not to worry if you don't hear from me for a while," Victor told him.

"I worry about you all the time," Tanner confessed. "Watch your back."

"I always do."

Victor hung up, and Tanner dropped his phone into his pocket before he folded his arms on the desk. After resting his head on his forearms, he closed his eyes. A strange feeling of sadness swamped him. Why did he have the weirdest notion he wouldn't be hearing from Victor ever again?

"Stupid. Victor will stay in touch. He's not going anywhere. Not yet at least," Tanner muttered. "Now get your ass back to work."

He straightened before turning back to study the report he'd been looking at when Victor called.

Chapter Nine

Victor raised his gaze from his computer screen when Bieito entered his office. He watched as Bieito rolled the sleeves of his shirt down then fastened them. Bieito's knuckles were scraped and bruised, but he didn't look as though he'd taken any injury during the interrogation.

Not that he expected anything like that. Bieito had learned from the best how to deliver the most damage without taking any. His father had been a master at that. Victor remembered watching Bieito's father get answers from people the elder Delarosa determined were enemies.

"What have you learned?" He leaned back in the chair then folded his arms over his chest. "Does he know where they've taken Kemen?"

Bieito wandered over to the side bar before pouring himself a glass of whiskey. When he held it up, Victor shook his head. He wasn't interested in drinking right then, and he was willing to wait until Bieito was ready to tell him.

After the glass was empty, Bieito set it back on the tray then swiped his hand over his mouth. It was then that Victor noticed how his hands shook. He stood, moving around the desk to go to Bieito. Resting his hand on the man's shoulder, he squeezed it tight for a second. It was as though his touch was exactly what Bieito needed.

"Apparently, this guy actually took the other guy's girlfriend, so it was revenge that made our man tell us about him." Bieito shook his head. "I remember when we'd just kill someone who stole our girlfriends."

"Did you ever have a girlfriend?" He frowned, trying to bring up a memory of seeing Bieito with a girl.

Bieito snorted. "Hell no. I wasn't about to get in trouble with one of them and end up married. It would've broken her heart, plus I didn't want to deal with the questions of why I wasn't attracted to her. Wasn't interested in living a lie."

Victor sighed. "Yet we're living a lie every minute," he said.

"Yes, we are, but while we might not be able to be open about it, we can be together when we're alone. I'll take that any day over not being able to have even that." Bieito covered Victor's hand for a second then stepped away.

"How connected was this guy?" Returning to his chair, he glanced at Bieito before sitting. Bieito's chuckle drew his attention again. "What's so funny?"

"He was very well connected. He's the man in charge of Cortez's heroin distribution throughout the southwestern United States." Bieito dropped into the chair across from him.

Victor raised his eyebrows in surprise. "Really? Did you ask Valdez's man why he didn't tell us this before now? We could've used this connection sooner."

Rolling his eyes, Bieito said, "He was worried we'd think he was a spy. I reassured him that wouldn't have happened, but not to hide things like this from us again."

"Good. What did Cortez's guy have to say?"

"I have to admit it wasn't that difficult to get the information from him. Cortez must not have any idea how big a coward the guy is, or else he'd have dumped him a long time ago. No pain tolerance. A few punches and he was spilling his guts." Bieito pulled a paper from his pants pocket then handed it to Victor. "I'll be calling our associates in Arizona to have them start looking."

Victor read the information and shook his head. "They took him over the border. How did they manage that?"

"Same way we smuggle drugs and people across, I assume."

"It was a rhetorical question," he informed his lover then smiled. "Did he know exactly where they were taking him?"

Bieito gestured toward the paper. "He said they were following the heroin route he'd set up. He doubted they would take him all the way to California, so Kemen should be held somewhere in Phoenix. Once I alert our men, they'll spread out around the city, see what they can find. They'll know where Cortez is strongest and where his base is."

Victor set the list on the files then pursed his lips while he thought. "How soon will we be leaving?"

"I've already talked to Valdez and he's gathering the men we'll take with us. We can get weapons once we're over the border." Bieito rubbed his forehead. "The money is here, so it'll be coming with us. They'll think we're there for the exchange. Once you ascertain that Kemen is still alive, we'll move in and take them down."

Nodding, Victor reached for the intercom and buzzed the kitchen. He ordered dinner for both of them to be brought directly to his office. When that was done, he settled back. "Do you think we should leave tonight or go first thing in the morning?"

"We have to go now. I've made sure the agent we've bought will be working. We'll get across using fake passports." Bieito closed his eyes.

"Why don't you lie down on the couch and rest until the food is here?" Victor suggested. "I've got some work to finish up before we go."

Bieito stood then wandered over to the leather couch up against the other wall. He kicked off his shoes before lying back against the cushions. Victor strolled to him, grabbing the blanket off the back of the couch then covering Bieito with it. He brushed some strands of hair off Bieito's forehead.

"I haven't seen you like this before. You've never been upset after questioning someone," he said softly.

The weariness in Bieito's gaze when he met Victor's touched him. "I've been doing this for a long time, Victor. I guess I'm just tired today. I didn't sleep much last night and I'm worried about your son."

Leaning down, he placed a gentle kiss on Bieito's lips. "Try to get some rest. The next couple of days are going to be very long and far more dangerous than we've dealt with before. I'm sure the world won't implode while you sleep."

"Asshole," Bieito muttered, his eyes already closing.

"That's probably true, but you like me, so you'll forgive me," Victor teased as he straightened then returned to his work.

* * * *

An hour later, Victor woke Bieito after the maids had laid dinner out for them. It wasn't the first time they'd eaten in his office. Bieito pushed the blanket off then joined him. He studied his lover. While Bieito didn't look as tired, he also didn't look as intense as he usually did either.

"I see the cook made all of your favorites," Bieito joked as they filled their plates.

"Of course, she did. I *am* the one who signs her paycheck," he pointed out, pouring out some wine.

Bieito grinned but didn't reply. They ate in silence, having spent so much time together they didn't need to fill the air between them with words. Victor finished eating first, setting his fork down onto his plate before picking up his wine glass.

He kept his gaze on the deep red liquid and said, "What if I told you I'm thinking about getting out of this business?"

Snorting, Bieito wiped his mouth with a napkin. "You're joking, right?"

Victor shrugged, feeling Bieito's curious gaze on him. "Maybe I am. Haven't you ever dreamed of doing something — anything — other than this?"

"Sure. Every kid wants to be something other than what his father was at some point in his childhood, but I wasn't going to go and do anything that was going to take me away from you." Bieito tapped the table with his fingers.

It was a nervous habit he had that Victor was pretty sure no one else knew about. Bieito would never allow anyone, besides Victor, to know one of his tells. *Is he nervous because he's worried how I'll react, knowing he's loved me for decades?* He wanted to reassure Bieito that it was all right. Victor had known Bieito loved him from the moment their eyes met when Bieito returned from college. It was the only reason why Victor had risked his father's anger by starting a relationship with Bieito.

"Are you regretting not staying with Esperanza and Kemen instead of coming home and taking over the business?"

Victor burst out laughing. "No. I don't regret that, but you and I both know I had no choice in the matter. I was taking over the cartel whether I wanted to or not. My father didn't let my mother go just so his eldest son would get a job as an accountant somewhere."

"An accountant? I know your degree is in business, but there's no way you'd survive as a pencil pusher. You'd be running whatever company you worked at within days of you getting hired." Bieito grinned. "You've got a mind for business and the kind of personality that gets people to work for you."

"You mean I have a last name and a reputation scary enough for people to do whatever I want because they're afraid I'll have them killed if they don't," Victor reminded him.

Inclining his head, Bieito agreed, "There is that, as well."

After drinking the rest of his wine, Victor put the glass down before standing. He gestured for Bieito to follow him as he moved to the couch then patted the cushion next to him. Bieito sat as close as he could without sitting on Victor's lap.

He took Bieito's hand in his, running his thumbs over his scraped knuckles. "I think the reason I asked you about wishing you'd done something else with your life is because I'm exhausted by all this shit.

There's a little voice inside of me telling me there's something different out in the world. Aren't you tired of always looking over your shoulder?"

Not caring if someone walked in on them, he leaned into Bieito's side and sighed when Bieito wrapped his arm around his shoulders. He stared at their entwined fingers. *God, I'm pathetic. Having Kemen kidnapped has turned me from a monster into a wuss. I need to suck it up before someone else besides Bieito figures out how weak I am right now.*

"I am. I've been tired of it all since your father died and you took over the entire operation. There's always been a fear inside me that someone will come to kill you, and I won't be able to do anything to stop them," Bieito admitted.

Taking a deep breath, Victor pushed away from Bieito then climbed to his feet. "All right. You need to go talk to Valdez and make sure he has everything in order. I'll go pack a small bag for both of us."

Bieito shot him a quick glance, a question in his eyes, but he didn't ask it. He nodded then left. Victor waited until he'd shut the door behind him before he dug a phone out of his desk drawer. He needed to make a quick call then he'd go up to his room and pack a bag.

* * * *

"Everything is ready," Bieito told Victor when he joined them in the foyer thirty minutes later. "I have our passports and other papers in case he checks us."

"He shouldn't, considering how much I pay him to turn his eye," Victor commented, walking past the men without acknowledging them.

He's back to his old self. Bieito bit his lip to keep from smiling. He should've known Victor would revert back to being a bastard at some point. Wallowing in pity wasn't in Victor's make-up. He usually shoved his way through the world, expecting it to change for him instead of changing himself.

"Gentlemen," Bieito said. "Let's get going. The plane is fueled and waiting for us."

"Yes, boss."

Valdez motioned for the others to head out where Victor stood next to the second SUV, obviously impatient to leave. He glared at all of them as they filed out. Bieito opened the door for him.

"Here you go, sir."

Victor growled under his breath as he slid into the seat. Bieito joined him then settled back against the leather. "No reason to be impatient. The plane is waiting. We'll get up to Mariposa in no time, and I'll contact our man in the CBP."

Frowning, Victor didn't reply, just stared out of the window. Bieito shook his head then tapped their driver on the shoulder. "Go."

"Yes, boss."

Twenty minutes later, they were pulling up to the private airport Victor used to fly in and out of the capital and the surrounding area. Victor boarded while Bieito double-checked everything to make sure they didn't have any problems before they took off.

When he got on the plane and took his place next to Victor, his head ached and he dug out a bottle of aspirin. He shook out two pills then accepted the glass of water Victor held out.

"Thanks," he murmured, washing the aspirin down.

"You're welcome." Victor leaned back. "We won't have any trouble landing in Mariposa?"

He cleared his throat. "No. I called our guy there. He's sending some of his men out to make sure the runway is clear. No authorities have been seen in the area either. They'll keep an eye out, and if it looks like someone's waiting for us, he'll radio the pilot and we'll land somewhere else. We have a couple other options if we need them."

Nodding, Victor fell silent and Bieito was happy about that. He still needed to work some details out. If—for some reason—their guy in the CBP couldn't be there to help them cross, he'd have to come up with something else. He wanted to make sure there were other ways for them to get into the States if needed.

Chapter Ten

Snap glanced over at Dalton. "Our informant called earlier. Seems there's two different illegal groups trying to cross later on tonight."

"Who the hell is this guy?" Dalton dropped into his chair with a grunt. "He's given us information on all the different cartels, not just Cortez. He has to be a higher up in one of them, but why hit his own people?"

Shrugging, Snap wrote down the last bit of details his informant had given him. "Maybe he has a bone to pick with his bosses and this is the way he gets back at them. How am I supposed to know? All I know is that he gave us the stuff to find Ken, so I'm not inclined to drive myself crazy about why he's turning on his own."

"Are we going out with Amirez and the CBP to find these guys? Did he say there might be drugs coming across with them?" Dalton fidgeted with a pencil.

"Yeah. I want to swing by my place quick to check on Ken then we can head down to Brownsville." Snap pushed to his feet. "I'm going to tell Penn about this."

"I'll go get our vests and a car. Meet you downstairs in a few." Dalton left while Snap made his way to his supervisor's office.

Once Penn gave him the okay to go, Snap grabbed his jacket off the back of his chair before making his way down to meet up with Dalton. He tried getting a hold of Ken to let him know he was coming home, but Ken's phone went to voicemail. Worry fought to take hold in his chest. Snap pushed it down.

"Ken not answering?" Dalton asked as they pulled into traffic.

"Yeah. He probably just fell asleep and doesn't have the phone near him." Snap hated how he tended to panic when he couldn't reach Ken. He knew it was residual fear left over from Ken being taken by the cartel.

Ken had been healing well from his injuries, plus he'd been getting to know Tanner, which made both Snap and Mac happy. They were all family now.

"Have you heard anything about Delarosa and Perez? Or are they keeping their heads down in Mexico?" Dalton stopped at a red light then glanced over at Snap.

"They'd disappeared, the last I heard. No one's seen them on their compound or in the capital where they were spotted two days ago." Snap grimaced as he stared out of the windshield. "Have to admit that makes me nervous."

Dalton hummed in agreement. "Yeah, though they could just have gone somewhere to hide out for a while. The Mexican army has turned the heat up on the cartels. It's not like they don't have the resources. Hell, they could have gone farther south."

Snap pursed his lips then shook his head. "No. Delarosa isn't the kind to run away. He believes he's above the law and we'll never catch him. But we got Perez."

"We didn't keep him, though," Dalton pointed out. "Ow!" He rubbed his shoulder where Snap had punched him. "Why'd you hit me?"

"You're just rubbing it in," Snap complained. "We didn't keep him this time. Next chance we get, we'll nail both of them and make it stick."

And deal with the fallout afterward. He didn't want to think about how Tanner would take it when Delarosa got arrested. Snap knew it was only a matter of time before they built a strong enough case to go take the man down. He had no doubt Ken wouldn't care one way or the other. His lover had no emotional attachment to Delarosa, only seeing him as the man who ran a drug cartel, which made him evil in Ken's eyes.

His phone buzzed and he saw it was Ken responding to his voicemail. "Apparently, he's over at Tanner's house, so we don't need to go see him. Let's head on down to Brownsville. I'll talk to him while we're on the road."

Dalton muttered but managed to work his way around to the highway then got on it in the right direction. They began planning out that night's mission.

* * * *

"Now that we're here, do we have any news about Kemen and where they're holding him?" Victor glared at Bieito, annoyed that they'd had to fly across the border and risk getting spotted by the CBP during the night. "Also, you send someone to talk to the border agent. He's not supposed to say he can't do it when we ask him for something."

"Yes, sir."

He watched as Bieito made a note, not that the man probably hadn't already contacted someone about the agent while they'd been driving to the safe house. Victor started pacing around the room while Bieito simply stood in the middle of it.

"Well?" he asked.

"Andrew just texted me, sir. He'll be here in five minutes and will tell us what he's found out. I wouldn't be surprised if they're keeping Kemen somewhere out in the desert. They probably have a compound much like this one out there." Bieito waved his hand, obviously encompassing the entire property with the vague gesture.

He shot Bieito a shocked glance. "You mean you don't know? I thought you knew everything there was to find out about our enemies."

"You're being a bastard," Bieito mentioned as though in passing. "I could find out for sure, but it would take more time than we have for me to dig through all of my files on the Cortez cartel, especially since Andrew is almost here and he can tell us."

Victor knew he was being an asshole, but he couldn't help the feeling that with each minute passing, Kemen was closer to death. "You do realize if we have to go in and rescue him, it'll be a firefight on American soil. The Americans won't let us get away with it."

Bieito lifted one shoulder in a haphazard shrug. "As long as Kemen is safe, I don't think it'll matter one way or the other. You know it's only a matter of time before they collect enough evidence and witnesses to come after us. This will give them exactly what they need, and we'll have the army knocking on our door in Mexico."

He spoke the truth.

"Have you made arrangements for Kemen to be taken somewhere safe?"

"Of course. The moment the young man is free, you and he will be taken to a waiting plane that will fly you to your island in the Caribbean. There you should be able to hide out long enough to discuss the family business with him and let him know where all your legitimate money is." Bieito held up the tablet he'd been typing on. "I've already sent you all the account information and passwords to a different email address. There's no way the DEA—or any of them— will know it's yours."

Narrowing his eyes, Victor stalked closer to Bieito. "Why would I need all of that? You'll be with us."

Bieito's smile held a hint of sadness at first before it morphed into a smirk. "Who do you think will be covering your ass while you're running for the hills? You'll need someone you trust to watch your back."

A sharp protest built in his chest, but Victor clamped down on it. As much as he wanted to say no and order Bieito to come with him, he knew he couldn't do that—not right then. Victor had a plan for the three of them. Unfortunately, he still needed time to work out the kinks, and time was the one thing he didn't have much of anymore.

Valdez knocked on the edge of the doorframe and waited until Victor motioned for him to come before walking in. Behind him came a skinny, blond man who seemed rather nervous and twitchy.

"Andrew?" Bieito studied the man, who nodded. "Thanks, Valdez. You go through the weapons we have available. Make sure they're ready. I'll have someone come get you when we're done here."

"Sure, boss." Valdez bowed to Victor then left.

"Come here." Bieito crooked his finger at Andrew. "This is Señor Victor Delarosa, your employer."

"Holy shit!" Andrew stared wide-eyed at Victor. "I hoped to never meet you, dude."

Victor rolled his eyes. "And believe me, the feeling is entirely mutual. I had no interest in ever learning your name or seeing your face."

Andrew blinked at Victor's harsh words. He opened his mouth to say something and Bieito cut him off.

"I asked you to gather some information for me. What have you got?" Bieito grabbed a hold of Andrew's arm then dragged him over to a chair before pushing him down onto it.

Licking his lips and rubbing his hands together, Andrew stared at them both. Victor swore he could see the man's brain struggling to organize everything.

"How much cocaine did you smoke before you came here?" He stepped right into Andrew's personal space.

"I didn't do any of that." Andrew's protest was weak and unbelievable.

Victor twisted his hand into the front of Andrew's dirty, hooded sweatshirt then shook the man hard. He probably would've kept on doing it for a while, except Bieito touched him lightly on the shoulder.

"Sir, he doesn't have many brain cells left. I think shaking him like that might dislodge what he does have. We need the information he has for us. Then I'll have Valdez and the men teach him a lesson about sampling our product instead of selling it." Bieito's calm voice cut through all of Victor's emotions, and he flung Andrew back into his seat.

Andrew held up his hands as though to ward off another attack. "Oh no. I don't use your shit. I'm square with you."

Bieito tilted his head to look at the scrawny man. "Then you must be using Cortez's stuff. I know you're working for both of us, trying to make money any way you can."

Victor poked Bieito in the biceps. "You knew he worked for the other cartels?"

"Yes. Why do you think I chose him to go find out where they're keeping Kemen? He's already a known entity with them. It should've been easy for him to get what we needed."

"It was. It totally was, man. They had no idea I was fishing for clues on that Kemen guy," Andrew bragged.

"Somehow I doubt that," Victor muttered as he stepped away. "You don't strike me as the James Bond type."

The guy frowned as though he were trying to figure out who James Bond was. Victor gestured to Bieito to get on with the questioning. If Victor had to deal with Andrew much longer, he'd strangle him on general principle.

"Focus, Andrew. Where are they keeping Kemen?" Bieito stood right in front of Andrew, so the man had to look up at him and he was all the guy could see.

Victor coughed to cover his laugh as Andrew's face paled and he visibly shook with fear, which was something Bieito was good at inspiring in others. And with good reason, though Victor was getting the feeling Bieito had lost all enthusiasm for his job.

"They have a large compound, south, about two hours out of town. I wrote down the directions." Andrew's hand shook as he held out a paper.

"They seriously let you see where they were going?" Victor asked.

Andrew nodded. "Oh yeah, man." At the kick to his foot from Bieito, Andrew amended it. "Sir. But it was a while ago that they let me go there. I didn't go yesterday, but I overheard a few of the enforcer dudes saying they'd brought a special guest up from Mexico a couple of days ago. Security's been beefed up at the place."

Bieito took the paper from Andrew, unfolded it then handed it off to Victor. "What else can you tell us? Anything about how many men might be at the compound? What kind of security they have?"

Wrinkling his nose as he thought, Andrew finally shook his head. "No, sir. The only time I've been there, they made me wear a blindfold until I got inside one of the buildings. It was just one of their packaging areas, so I didn't see nothing."

"Figures." Victor read the directions to the Cortez compound and nodded. "He can go since he doesn't have anything else to tell us."

Bieito yanked Andrew out of the chair then dragged him to the door. After opening it, he motioned to one of the guards standing in the hallway. "Take this man to Valdez and tell him that Andrew needs to be reminded what happens when he uses the product he sells."

"Wait. I told you I don't use your shit," Andrew protested, struggling in Bieito's grip.

"This is just a lesson to make sure you remember never to do that. Cortez would kill you if he figured out you were sampling the cocaine," Bieito informed him as he handed him off to the guard. "Also, let Valdez know I'll need him for a meeting in about two hours. He can come here."

"Yes, boss." The guard hauled Andrew away while Bieito turned back to Victor.

Victor crumpled the paper in his hand. "What do we do now? We can't go in there blind without any kind of idea about their firepower and men."

Bieito pinched his bottom lip as he seemed to be thinking. "I have a resource I can tap. I haven't used her before, but I think this might be the best reason to do it."

"Her?"

"A friend I made while at college here in the States. We've stayed in touch throughout the years and she works in FBI." Bieito didn't sound convinced about contacting her. "She doesn't know who I really am, since I didn't use my real name when I attended the university."

Victor snickered as he propped his ass on the edge of the desk behind him. "Do you really think she hasn't figured your true identity out by now? If she hasn't, she's not very observant. I'm pretty sure your picture has been passed around the Bureau, along with mine, on the list of their top ten most wanted."

Shrugging, Bieito said, "She might have, and has continued the friendship to gather information on us, but I've never put anything in my emails to her about the cartel or what I do for you. I don't even use an email associated with me."

Victor trusted Bieito. If the man thought this mysterious woman could get them information about Cortez's compound then he'd go along with him. "Go and call her. See what she can get us."

As much as he wanted to ask what kind of relationship Bieito had with her, he remembered his lover mentioning he'd never been romantically involved with a woman. Victor conceded he had no room for jealousy toward this woman when he'd had a child with Esperanza and never told Bieito about it.

Bieito nodded before leaving. Victor began pacing again, taking deep breaths to calm his impatience. While his paternal instinct was to rush in and rescue Kemen, every other inclination in Victor told him they had to plan things out. Cortez had to know Victor would try to free Kemen without paying a cent of the ransom. Little did the bastard realize Victor would give him his entire fortune as long as Kemen was released without being harmed.

Being cautious was what had kept Victor alive and out of prison for so long. And even if he were to rush off, Bieito would stop him, because Bieito's first priority was to keep Victor out of harm's way. That compulsion was ingrained in Bieito's DNA—or at least Victor thought that sometimes.

Chapter Eleven

"Thank you, Carla. I appreciate any help you can give me," Bieito said after explaining to her why he needed the information.

"I'm not sure how much help I can be, Ben, and you do realize I'm going to have to report this to my supervisor? I'll get a reprimand for it as well, since I did it without their permission." Carla's unhappiness could be heard over the phone and Bieito wished he hadn't had to involve her.

Bieito wandered around the bedroom he'd ducked into to make the call. "I know, honey, and I'm so sorry to ask you for this. I didn't have anyone else to turn to."

Well, he did, but he wasn't about to get Pablo and Mac mixed up in the problem. They were already walking a thin line by not reporting Pablo's relationship to Victor. If the Feds found out Mac—or Pablo—had helped them, they would end up in jail just as fast as Bieito and Victor would.

"I know your boss though, and if you explain who this information was for, he'll let it go," he informed her, having already discussed it with the man above her. It helped to have several government agents on the payroll. He hadn't told the man who he was contacting, just that he was getting some files on the Cortez cartel and whoever came to inform him about it wasn't to get in trouble. Hell, Bieito made sure his bribes were higher than they could get elsewhere.

"You know my boss? Just who the hell are you, Ben?" She sounded annoyed now.

His laugh was filled with disgust at himself. "Trust me. You don't want to know the truth, Carla. Plus it's better if you don't. Plausible deniability. It might help you in the end, though I promise if you do, I'll make sure you have the best lawyer in the country."

"That's supposed to reassure me?" She huffed. "Never mind. I'm sending you all the files we have on the Cortez cartel and what we know about their movements in Arizona. There are other files from the DEA. Looks like they've had that particular place under surveillance for a year or so too."

Relief rushed through him for a few seconds. He hated going into any situation blind, and they wouldn't have time to do any kind of recon of the area. Time was running out for Kemen, and Bieito didn't want to think of how Victor would react if his son was murdered.

"Thank you again, honey, and if there's ever anything I can do for you, don't hesitate to ask me. I'm in your debt."

"You are, and when I lose my job for this, I expect you to support me for the rest of my life."

"Deal." He would do it because he did understand exactly what he'd asked her to do for him. It wasn't like he didn't have more than enough money to support her and himself if he were to stop working for the cartel right then and there. "I have to go."

She sighed. "Be careful. I know whatever you're planning is dangerous, and as angry as I am at you right now, I don't want you dead. Now I need to get back to work so I can break the law for you."

He ended the call then dropped to the edge of the bed, letting his hands hang between his knees. When had asking—or making—someone to break the law caused a crisis of conscience for him? It wasn't like he hadn't done it for more years than he could count without having any qualms.

Reaching out to Carla had been the hardest thing he'd done. Maybe it was simply because their friendship had never been tainted by the cloud of his working for the cartel. There had been something pure about it, yet now it would never be the same, and he regretted it.

Taking a deep breath, he stiffened his spine before standing. He didn't have time to pity himself for the monster he'd become. He had a young man to save and a lover to keep from self-destructing. Maybe when the whole problem was over, he'd be able to find a quiet corner and cry for a while.

The funny thing was his father would've been proud of how he was handling the situation while his mother would be so disappointed in him. Elizabeth Perez had loved her husband, but she'd had no illusion about the kind of man he was. Bieito knew his mother had always hoped her son would turn out differently. Hell, he'd overheard her many times praying late at night that God would direct his path somewhere else.

What other choice did he have when his heart had fallen in love with the boss's son and would accept no other in his place? Bieito had been doomed from the first moment he'd laid eyes on Victor. While it had been a dangerous and difficult life, he had no regrets for what he'd done to keep Victor safe.

"Did you get a hold of the lady?" Victor spoke from the doorway.

"Yes. She's going to send me the files I need, then go tell her supervisor she did it." He scrubbed his hand over his face. "Fortunately, her supervisor is on our payroll, so he'll tell her it's okay. I should have the specs and details within the hour."

Victor walked up to him then cradled his face with his hands. "I'm sorry you had to ask her. I can tell it was hard on you."

"What can I do about it? We need the information and she can get it for us. It's not like I haven't done worse over the years." He nuzzled Victor's palm for a moment then stepped back. "Apparently, she has some surveillance reports from the DEA about Cortez as well. They'll be part of the package she sends."

Victor didn't stop him as he moved around the man then headed out of the bedroom. He made his way to the office where he went right to the laptop he'd set on the desk. After turning it on and loading his email, he flopped into the chair to wait. Bieito glanced up when Victor set a glass of water next to his elbow.

"Drink this while I see what I can get made to eat. Not sure if they have any food in this place," Victor muttered as he strolled away.

Bieito couldn't help smiling. No one would ever believe how nurturing Victor was when they were alone. More often than not, he would take care of Bieito, making sure he didn't miss meals and got enough sleep. It was kind of sad Victor could only show that side of him when there wasn't anyone else around to see.

A ding told him an email had arrived. Checking, he saw Carla's name on the screen and clicked on the attachment. The size of the file made him cringe, but he started it downloading. Movement by the door had him looking up. Valdez stood there.

"I know it's not time yet, but I wanted to let you know we took care of Andrew. We're keeping him in one of the back rooms for now. Don't want to take a chance of him running to Cortez to tell him anything." Valdez cracked his knuckles. "I don't trust him any farther than I can throw him."

Bieito snorted. "Good job. I forgot to tell you to keep him around, so thanks for taking the initiative on that. I'm getting specs and security for Cortez's compound. Once Señor Delarosa and I go over it, I'll bring you in and we can figure out what our approach is going to be."

Valdez nodded. "Too bad we can't just go in with guns blazing and wipe them all out."

"If we were in Mexico, we could do that, since the Cortez compound isn't near a major city. We'd be in and out before the army arrived. The Americans frown on things like that here, and they'll be armed to the teeth compared to us." Bieito shook his head. "I'd prefer to get in and out without firing a shot, but we know that won't happen."

"Maybe we can keep the body count to a minimum," Victor suggested as he walked in, carrying a tray of covered plates. He looked at Valdez. "There's food in the kitchen for you and the others. Apparently, one of the ladies who lives here took it upon herself to order takeout for us."

Valdez bowed. "Thank you, sir."

After he left, Victor set the tray down then gestured for Bieito to fill his plate first. "You need to eat. Your headache isn't going to get any better if you starve yourself."

"Have you heard anything more about the ransom? We brought the money with us, thinking they would have us bring it to them here, but now I'm wondering if they mean for us to drop it off somewhere else."

He saw Victor lift one shoulder in a shrug. "We'll deal with that when we come to it. I'm not worried about the money right now. I want to make sure Kemen is safe then we'll take care of the bastards who thought kidnapping my son was a smart decision."

Which meant wiping out the Cortez cartel and removing any threat to Kemen. Bieito had no doubt that when they got back to Mexico, Victor would declare an all-out war against Cortez. There would be a river of blood flowing through the country with Victor avenging the insult to his family. Bieito would be with him the entire way.

Another ding and Bieito put down his fork to open the first file. Aerial photographs began appearing on the screen. He silently thanked Carla for her thoroughness. "We hit the mother lode with these," he told Victor. "We have pictures of the compound. It'll tell us how many buildings there are. Also, we have close-ups of the different men coming and going from the area."

He drew in a breath, causing Victor to give him a sharp look.

"What is it?"

"Kemen is there, sir." Bieito isolated one photo then turned the laptop toward Victor. "I assume this is him."

The young man in the picture looked exactly like Victor had at twenty. Bieito saw Victor trace the lines of Kemen's face with his gaze.

"I haven't seen any recent pictures of him," Victor admitted. "I just got updates from the man I had keeping an eye on him and his mother."

"He looks exactly like you and Pablo," Bieito said.

Victor laughed. "It seems as though the Delarosa genes dominate when it comes to reproduction. I believe Kenneth looks much like we do as well."

Bieito hummed. "If I remember correctly, he does. Your father was the kind of man who would've been arrogant enough to be proud of the fact that his sons resembled him. Also, that his grandson is just as handsome."

Rolling his eyes, Victor said, "I never told my father about Kemen. I was afraid if he knew, he'd force Esperanza to come live on the compound with us. I've never wanted this life for Kemen. He deserves a good life like Pablo has—one where he's not always looking over his shoulder for enemies or law enforcement."

"He'll continue to live the life you've given him. This is all a small detour, a bit of an adventure he'll be able to brag about when he's older. The women will fall all over him while he tells it." Bieito chuckled. "Of course, he won't tell them his family runs one of the largest drug cartels in the world. That might be a bit of a turn off to the smart ones."

"Or he'll collect the ones looking for a rich man to support them while they spend all of his money," Victor commented as he settled back in his seat to continue eating.

Bieito wiggled his head. "True. Did that happen to you while you were at the university? Did the girls know who you were?"

Victor chewed then swallowed before he said, "Oh yes, they did know who I was. My father wasn't afraid of the Mexican authorities. He wasn't about to have me lie about my name. Besides, at the time, I wasn't doing anything with the business, so they couldn't arrest me for it."

"Right, plus your father had the police on his payroll as well. Life was much easier back then. Everyone was willing to be bribed to look the other way. Not like today," he joked.

"Damn all these people suddenly finding their ethics and morals on us. Being a drug kingpin isn't what it used to be." Victor winked at him and they cracked up.

When their laughter subsided, they finished their meal then Bieito scrolled through the pictures before sending them to the printer for hard copies. He also went through the DEA surveillance reports to see if they'd figured out a schedule for the guards.

"I do love how thorough the DEA is. We have everything we need to make an organized attack. If God smiles on us, we might even be able to get out of this with limited causalities." He wasn't going to pray for no shots being fired. God didn't like them that much.

"All right. Get Valdez in here and we'll work up a detailed plan. Figure out where to place the men. We're only taking the ones we brought with us from Mexico. I'm not risking this mission blowing up in our faces because of some hotshot bragging to the wrong person." Victor gathered their plates. "I'll return this to the kitchen then be right back."

Bieito sent Valdez a text to get him into the office then went back to shuffle through the printouts, marking the ones they needed and setting aside the ones he deemed not as important. They could always come back to those if they needed other specifics.

Victor and Valdez arrived at the same time and they got down to business. Once the whole mission was planned, it was late at night, causing Victor to make the decision that they'd execute it the next night. It needed to be under the cover of darkness as much as possible, so the DEA—who they assumed were still watching the place since they had current pictures of Kemen—wouldn't notice them as quickly.

Bieito sent Valdez off to bed. "We'll start gathering all the weapons and other items we need tomorrow. That'll give us a chance to get some things we might have from our other storage buildings."

Valdez left and Victor waited while Bieito shut down the laptop then locked all of it in the safe for the rest of the night. They weren't taking any chances since they were out of their element here on American soil.

"Let's go to bed, Bieito," Victor said, holding his hand out to him.

"Here?" Bieito hesitated, not sure he should take it when there might still be people about.

"Yes. The guards are all outside. Everyone else is in bed. No one will see us. Also, my bedroom is far enough away, no one will hear anything." Victor grabbed his hand then tugged, encouraging him to move.

He wasn't about to say no to Victor. He hadn't expected to have any sex until after the mission was over. *Maybe Victor wants to blow off some steam before the excitement starts.* Whatever his lover's reasons were, he wasn't going to complain.

Chapter Twelve

Victor shut the door behind them, making sure it was locked, before he turned to smile at Bieito. "You have no idea how turned on I get watching you plot missions. All the talk about guns, bullets, point men and who's going to be bringing up the rear."

"Gets you hot, huh?" Bieito reached out to press his palm against the front of Victor's pants.

"Oh yes," he practically purred as he arched his back, trying to get more friction against his cock.

"I should take advantage of that," Bieito said, dropping to his knees while working on opening Victor's belt and pants.

Victor didn't help him, but he didn't fight him either. He simply ran his fingers through Bieito's dark hair and played with the curls at the nape of Bieito's neck. "You need a haircut," he commented.

Bieito grinned. "Been too busy the past couple of days to schedule an appointment. When we get back home, I'll have Maria trim it."

Humming, Victor didn't say anything. He loved the feel of the soft strands falling through his fingers. He gasped when the cool air hit his heated flesh then moaned when Bieito wrapped his lips around his shaft. Victor fought against the urge to shove as deep as he could get into Bieito's mouth, not wanting to choke his lover.

He spread his legs, constricted by the fabric around his knees. Bieito cupped Victor's balls before playing with them while he slowly began to bob up and down along Victor's length. Bieito scraped his sharp teeth over Victor's sensitive skin and he twitched a little, drawing a low chuckle from Bieito.

"Watch yourself," he warned, tugging hard on a lock of Bieito's hair. "And make sure you don't make me come. I want to fuck you."

A quick glance up was all the acknowledgment he needed. Bieito would play and tease for a little while but wouldn't take him over the edge.

Suddenly, Bieito pulled off him and Victor growled his displeasure. Bieito pushed to his feet.

"I think this would be more comfortable for you if we were both naked on the bed." Bieito nodded toward the large, four-poster bed Victor had been surprised to see in the safe house when he'd arrived.

He stripped quickly then dashed across the floor to leap onto the mattress. A shocked laugh tore from him when he sank into the softness. "Definitely not firm like the one I have at home."

"You do realize you kicked some middle-level dealer out of his bed for the night, right?" Bieito asked as he divested himself of his own clothes.

Victor grimaced. "I hope they changed the sheets."

Tilting his head to one side, Bieito studied him. "That's really all you can think of?"

"I don't want to sleep in some nasty sheets, Bieito. You know how I am." Victor shuddered at the thought that someone might have sweated on the blankets and sheets he sat on.

Bieito tackled him back onto the bed then crushed their lips together. At the first touch of his body against Bieito's, Victor forgot about everything except getting more of that amazing feeling. He moaned when Bieito rubbed his groin over Victor's. All that hot, hard flesh covered with velvety soft skin.

"No," he protested when Bieito eased away from him, shivering a little at the cool air washing over his flushed skin. Then he jerked when Bieito blew a puff of hot breath over his cock before taking it into his mouth again.

"I should get a fucking trophy for restraint every time we're in a room together. How I manage not to make you blow me is beyond me." He thrashed his head from side to side as Bieito applied more and more suction with each bob of his head.

Bieito slid off a few inches. "Such a sweet talker," he teased.

"Fuck you, Bieito. Get back to what you're good at—sucking my dick." Victor mock-glared at him, knowing his use of crude language wouldn't insult Bieito.

"Yes, sir." And he did just as Victor had told him.

He planted his feet on the mattress then let them fall open to give Bieito as much access as he wanted to his body. While Bieito blew him, Victor pinched and tugged at his own nipples, making them hard and aching. He jerked slightly when Bieito pressed a finger into his ass. While he wasn't going to come until he was inside Bieito, he didn't object to a little ass play beforehand.

Victor relaxed as best he could and bit his bottom lip to keep from shouting when Bieito bumped his gland the first time. He must have made some sound because Bieito looked pleased with himself and began to work Victor's cock and ass hard. He was obviously determined to push Victor as close to the edge as he could without taking him over.

He lost himself in the sensations of fullness, heat and pressure. He let all of his worries about Kemen and their future go, to be thought about and gone over some other day. These stolen moments were for him and Bieito to spend time together without the weight of the world holding them back.

Pressure built behind his balls—a familiar indication his climax was close. He tapped Bieito on the shoulder. When those lust filled dark eyes met his, he inhaled. All of Bieito's emotions and needs shone in them, and Victor wondered if Bieito could see how he felt in his gaze.

"You need to stop. I'm going to come," he warned.

Bieito let his cock slide out, pausing to drop a gentle kiss on Victor's flared head before he flopped onto his back. Victor smiled fondly when Bieito grabbed his knees to pull them to his chest.

"I should get the lube," he said, trailing his finger down the underside of Bieito's erection, over his balls to his hole. He caressed the puckered opening and drew a shudder from his lover.

"No. Just fuck me, Victor. I don't mind the burn," Bieito pleaded in a desperate tone.

"I think we'll use a little," Victor insisted, scrambling off to go dig a bottle from his bag. After returning and settling between Bieito's thighs, he positioned his coated cock at Bieito's entrance. "Now relax and push out while I'm pushing in," he explained.

Bieito shot him a disgusted look. "I'm not a virgin, jackass. I know how to get fucked."

Victor blinked and Bieito grimaced. "You know what I mean."

"Yeah I do." Victor eased in an inch at a time. He almost held his breath until he popped through the ring of muscle then sank deep in Bieito's ass. Freezing when he bottomed out, he stared at Bieito, watching the man's every expression to make sure he wasn't hurting him.

There had been tension when he first started, but as Bieito adjusted to his intrusion, he relaxed under Victor until Bieito curled up to brush a kiss over his lips.

"You can move now," Bieito told him before lying back.

Victor gripped Bieito's hips then started slamming into him. He was no longer interested in being gentle or slow. All he wanted was heat, speed and pleasure. After having Bieito play with him, he was primed and ready to come. It wouldn't take long, but he had to hang on. He didn't want to climax before Bieito.

The sound of their bodies coming together filled the room, along with their moans and pants. Bieito arched his back, changing the angle of Victor's thrust then cried out Victor's name when he nailed the man's gland. Having the right place now, Victor hit it every stroke.

He lost his smooth rhythm as his climax overtook him and burned through his entire nervous system. He thrust in once more then flooded Bieito's inner passage with hot cum. He had one last thought that he hoped Bieito had come as well.

When Victor returned to himself, he found he'd collapsed on top of Bieito, and a cooling pool of cum was starting to stick them together. Bieito traced

Victor's spine with lazy circles while he stared up at the ceiling.

"I guess I don't have to ask if you enjoyed it," Victor muttered as he peeled away from Bieito.

Shooting him a happy smile, Bieito inquired, "Did you think I wouldn't?"

He shrugged, a little uncomfortable. "I didn't wait to make sure you got off before I came."

"Don't worry, Victor. Just the feeling of you spilling inside me was enough to shove me right over the edge." Bieito patted his shoulder. "I should go get a towel for us to wash off the mess."

Victor wanted to say no, but he couldn't find the strength, so he let Bieito climb out of bed while he flung his arm up to block his eyes from the sudden light.

"Fuck. Couldn't you find your way to the bathroom without the light?" he whined then smiled when he heard Bieito chuckle.

"I didn't come equipped with night vision, sir. So sorry to have damaged your precious retinas."

"Holy shit!" He jack-knifed up when a cold, wet cloth landed on his stomach. Glaring at Bieito, Victor wiped off then threw it back at Bieito. "Hurry up and get in bed. I'm tired."

"Jeezus," Bieito muttered. "I would've thought having your mind blown with great sex would've made you a little less grumpy. Apparently, I was wrong."

Victor immediately felt bad. He waited until Bieito rejoined him under the blankets before he took the man's hands in his. "I'm sorry. I loved what we just did. For a while, my brain shut off and I wasn't worried about anything except making sure you were enjoying yourself. But the moment my mind kicked back in, all I can think about is getting to Kemen and praying that you aren't hurt while we're doing it."

"I swear you have multiple personality disorder or something." Bieito squeezed his hands then patted his cheek. "You need to shut all of it off, Victor, or you're going to drive yourself crazy. Lie down and try to relax. The morning will be soon enough to freak out about all this shit."

He did as Bieito advised, wiggling until he found the perfect spot on the mattress then he tugged the sheets up to his chin. Bieito shifted at his side before throwing his arm over Victor's chest, pinning him down. He'd always thought he'd hate the feeling of being held down, but from the first time Bieito had done it, Victor had found he liked it. It was a way for him to let go of control.

"Trust me, Victor. Nothing is going to happen in the next couple of hours. I've got you," Bieito whispered in his ear, and Victor melted as though all of his muscles and bones had turned to wax.

Taking a deep breath, he let go of everything, allowing his eyes to close.

* * * *

The jarring sound of a phone ringing woke him some time later. He wasn't interested in opening his eyes, but he heard Bieito swear and climb out of bed then the rustle of clothes as Bieito must have been getting his cell out of a pocket.

"Perez," he growled into the phone.

Victor's cock stiffened at the rough sound of Bieito's voice. *Seriously, I have it bad when just his voice makes me hard.* Then he heard Bieito curse again before telling whomever was on the other end to call him back later in the morning so he could get more details.

When Bieito crawled in next to him again, Victor trembled at the chill emanating from Bieito's skin. Snuggling close, he wanted to warm him up.

"Who was that?"

"Our contact at the Brownsville port of entry," Bieito grumbled, seemingly not happy about being woken.

"Why would he call this late? Or early, I guess." He didn't check the clock on the dresser across the room to see how long they'd slept. Whatever time it was, it hadn't been long enough.

Bieito sighed as he rolled over onto his side to face Victor. "Do you really want to go over this now? Can't we talk about it when the sun has risen?"

"Now who's grumpy," Victor joked.

"He wanted to let me know the DEA and CBP nabbed two of our shipments last night. One of illegals and the other was about six hundred thousand dollars' worth of heroin." Bieito cleared his throat. "The only good thing is we had another three shipments get through, plus one transport of money back into Mexico. Also, it seems like we weren't the only ones to get hit. The other cartels had shipments intercepted as well."

Victor wanted to swear, yet he couldn't work up the usual anger for having his business disrupted like that. "The odds are skewed in our favor, you know. The more we throw at the border, the more likely a majority of it will get through. The CBP doesn't have the man power to catch all of what we're transporting across both ways."

He felt, more than saw, Bieito nod. "I know, but it's annoying. These last couple of months, it seems like they've been getting better at finding our stuff. It's almost like they can read our minds about where we're sending it through. Are we getting that predictable?"

"I have no real clue. Maybe once this is over with, we should sit and go over all the different routes and our usual schedule. We can come up with new ones, mix things up a little." He rested his hand on Bieito's chest. "Right now, I think we should take your advice. Let things go for now. We'll get some more sleep and deal with it later."

Bieito inched close to press a kiss onto his lips. "Good idea. Sleep well, Victor."

"You too," he said softly, enjoying how the even sound of Bieito's breathing lulled him to sleep.

Chapter Thirteen

"Something's going on," Snap muttered to Dalton as his partner sat at their joint desks.

Dalton took a sip of his coffee then frowned at him. "What are you talking about?"

"Penn's been in a meeting with some FBI agents since I got here this morning. There was some shouting earlier. Now everything has gotten ominously quiet." He grabbed the large coffee that Dalton shoved across the desk at him.

"You didn't press your ear to the door and eavesdrop?" Dalton held up his hands to ward off the ball of crumpled paper Snap threw at him. "Why are you so freaked out? It's not like the Feds have never come over here, yelling at us about something we did. One of our guys probably stepped on a FBI case or something like that. Penn will work it out, and they'll go back to their little ivory towers."

It had happened before and would probably happen again, but Snap couldn't shake the feeling that this was something far more important than just some bureaucratic posturing. He kept his ears peeled to pick up anything as he and Dalton began going through the mounds of paperwork they had to file for their busts the night before.

"It was a good haul," Dalton commented, after typing away for a few minutes.

"Yeah. Put a little dent into some of the cartels' business. It's interesting that he gave us information on three different cartels last night. Usually he only does one." Snap opened one of his drawers to dig out another notebook since the one he'd been using was full. He jotted down a few names the mules — the men transporting the heroin they'd confiscated last night — had given him. He'd check to see if they were known cartel men or if they were new people he would have to keep an eye on.

Dalton grunted. "Yeah. He seems to be upping his game since Ken's kidnapping. Maybe he's trying to make amends for what happened."

Snap rolled his eyes. "Why would he do that unless he had something to do with it? And how could he when no one knew Ken was working for us except you, me and Penn?"

"Well, Mac and Tanner knew as well," Dalton pointed out.

"Sure, but do you really think either of them would've told someone?"

Pursing his lips, Dalton pretended to think about it before he shook his head. "Nah. Just talking out of my ass. Maybe the dude knows something we don't and is trying to insure he does as much damage as he can before it happens."

That was a possibility. Snap wasn't sure he wanted to know what the man could know that would drive him to snitch on his fellow cartel people. If it was true, it had to be something serious because the cartels would kill a person for the slightest infraction and do it without even thinking twice.

Penn's door flew open and everyone watched as two red-faced men stalked from his office. They didn't look at anyone, just made their way to the elevators as quickly as possible. Penn stuck his head out to glance around.

"Jefferson. Grab your partner and get your ass in here," Penn ordered. He didn't wait to see if Snap obeyed.

"I guess we get to hear what all of this was about," Dalton murmured as they stood then strolled over to their supervisor's office.

"Shut the door," Penn told them as they entered.

Once it was done, he gestured for them to sit. "As you can see, I was graced with a visit from the local Special Supervisory Agent in Charge of the Houston field office and his second in command." Penn shook his head. "Usually, we don't have a problem with each other, but seems like there's been a leak in the Phoenix office and somehow it's been connected with us."

Snap frowned and Dalton looked just as confused.

"How are we connected? I don't know anyone who works for the Bureau in Phoenix," Snap said.

"Several files of surveillance photos were leaked to someone. They still haven't tracked who they went to, but they're working on it." Penn shoved a file at Snap. "This is all that they know so far."

Snap held it so both he and Dalton could read it. All the information gathered on the Cortez cartel, including several different DEA ops, had been leaked to an unknown person at some point during the last twenty-four hours.

The interesting part was that the DEA had had a compound two hours south of Phoenix under surveillance for over a year. They'd known it was owned by the Cortez cartel but hadn't been able to get enough evidence to raid it. So they'd kept on taking pictures, making notes of deliveries and interesting comings and goings about the place. These photos were part of the items that had leaked.

"Looks like someone was looking for everything they could find out about Cortez and his cartel," Snap remarked before handing the file back to Penn. "But I still don't see how it ties to us."

"There's been some rumors circulating the last week or so about tension between Delarosa and Cortez. Since we have the lead on the Delarosa drug case while the FBI is working on building a racketeering case against him, they wanted to know if we had anything to do with this leak." Penn sneered. "I told them my men weren't about to risk their jobs doing something as idiotic as giving a cartel information about a rival. They didn't seem to believe me."

Dalton rubbed his chin. "What would we have to gain by doing that? Aside from watching the explosion when Delarosa takes Cortez out. I mean, it would be kind of fitting and would give us one less cartel to worry about, but still, we don't gain anything from it."

After standing, Penn walked around his office. "We all know that. There's also been a rumor that Perez has been seen in Phoenix."

Snap straightened. "Really? How credible is the rumor? I didn't think Perez would risk showing his face in the States for a while. He has to let the dust filter back down after we picked him up."

"The agents seem to believe it's true. So here's what you're going to do. You two are flying to Phoenix to meet up with our agents out there. They'll take you to the compound to check it out, and you can do some digging around to see if Perez has somehow figured how to get across the border without being detained." Penn glared at them. "I'm getting fed up with the way Delarosa and his men act like they can just come and go from our country. When we catch them, we're going to nail their asses to the tree and make sure any charges brought against them stick."

"Yes, sir." Snap stood. "We'll go pack and catch the first flight out."

Penn dismissed them. They gathered their things from their desks then rushed down to their vehicles.

"I'll meet you at the airport a-sap," he told Dalton. "You know the drill."

"Pack light and fast," Dalton informed him. "We're going on an adventure."

Smiling, Snap shook his head. "I'm not sure how exciting this one will be. I'm not convinced Perez would come across the border when he knows we'll be keeping a sharp eye out for him."

"If he has, then something big must be going on." Dalton paused in the middle of climbing into his car then turned to look at Snap. "Do you think Delarosa is finally going after Cortez?"

"It's a war that's been brewing for a while. If it is about to happen, we missed the incident that ignited the flame. All we can hope for is that there isn't a lot of collateral damage when the dust settles." Snap shuddered to think of how many people could die if the two cartels went into all-out war with each other.

Dalton paled as well. "You're right. Let's hope that's not what's happening. I'll meet you at the airport."

They got into their separate vehicles and left to go home to pack.

* * * *

Bieito stood in the middle of the armory, running his gaze over the tables filled with automatic rifles, shotguns, handguns and even a rocket launcher. It always amazed him how much firepower they amassed at the different storage houses. A majority of these weapons had been earmarked for Mexico and the Delarosa cartel army down there. He just hadn't arranged the shipments for them yet. *Good thing I was running behind on that. We would've been scrambling if I had actually moved this stuff earlier, like I'd planned.*

"All right. There'll be ten of us going in." He nodded at Valdez. "Valdez, you and four of the others will take out the perimeter guards. You pick which ones you want with you. Try to do it quietly. I'd like to get as far as possible into this mission before the alarm is sounded."

Valdez nodded, slinging an AR-15 over his shoulder before he began to fill his pockets with extra magazines. There was a large Ka-Bar knife strapped to his thigh, and Bieito knew the man was really good with the blade.

"I'll take four men with me and start looking for our target. If you capture one of the guards without having to kill him, Valdez, see if you can get that information out of him. It'll make our job a lot easier. We can't be bungling around into every building, searching for him." Bieito pointed to three main buildings in the center of the compound. "My gut says he's in one of these three buildings. They're the hardest to approach without being seen and the easiest to defend."

He picked up his bulletproof vest, settling it over his shoulders before strapping it down using the Velcro fastenings. They were all dressed in black with paint smeared on their faces where their balaclava masks didn't cover their skin. He wouldn't pull his down until they'd exited the vehicles to make their way into the compound.

"I'll be waiting at the vehicles for you to return," Victor spoke up from where he stood, just out of the way in the corner of the room. He hadn't said anything while Bieito had explained the mission's objective and assigned positions to the men.

Bieito appreciated the show of faith it had been for Victor to do that. It wasn't that Victor didn't know how to plan raids and make strategy. It was more that it wasn't his job to do so. Bieito—as his right-hand man and the head of his security—was in charge of any kind of mission. He was the brawn to Victor's brains.

"I expect you to execute this raid with precision and with as minimal amount of blood lost as possible. At least on our side," Victor amended. "Remember I want Kemen Larenz untouched and alive. He's mine to deal with as I see fit. There will be swift punishment if this rule isn't obeyed."

"Yes, sir," they all said together.

Victor gestured for Bieito to continue. While Bieito finished giving the last few instructions, the men suited up, picking up their weapons of choice and making sure they had enough ammo to get them through a firefight. An extra crate full of guns and ammo was loaded into the back of one of the SUVs then Bieito decided they were ready.

Full night had fallen by the time they left their safe house. The good thing was that the house was far enough off the beaten path no one would have noticed all the activity around it, which was one of the reasons why Bieito had chosen it all those years ago when he'd been looking for houses in Phoenix to buy.

He climbed into the back seat of the second SUV with Victor next to him. Once they were on the road, he reached over the seat to tug a vest from where he'd stuffed it. "Here." He slapped it against Victor's chest.

"Seriously? I'm not going into the compound with you. I'll be perfectly safe with the vehicles." Victor tried to push it away, but Bieito wouldn't let him.

"No. You're going to wear it in case one of them gets past us and decides to take a shot at you." Bieito nodded toward their driver. "That's why Samuel here will be staying with you. He'll keep an eye on you."

Victor glared at him. "I can take care of myself. Your father and you both worked hard to ensure that."

Bieito leaned closer to Victor, almost pressing his lips against his ear. "It's not that I don't think you can take care of yourself. It's because I don't want you hurt in any way. You do know how that would destroy me, right?"

His confession did the work, and Victor subsided, putting the vest on without any more arguments. Bieito moved back to his original position, going over the entire mission again in his mind. The thing was, no matter how precisely he planned it, the whole mission would be fucked up within minutes of them entering the compound. It was the nature of a job like this.

The human element alone guaranteed they'd have to revise their movements throughout. Plus, he didn't have any clue whether the DEA would be watching the compound that night or not. And if they were, their agents were a whole other ball game and one he'd have to deal with very carefully. Unlike some of the cartels, the Delarosa family had always done their best not to kill law enforcement members. Even while Victor's father had run the cartel and believed he was invincible, he'd still chosen not to harm the men on the other side of the badge.

Bieito and Victor had carried on that tradition as best they could. Unfortunately, sometimes things happened and an undercover agent got killed. He liked to point out the man had been killed for other reasons, not because he'd been an agent. Not that it would erase the mark against him in Heaven.

Victor touched his knee and he glanced at him. "You'll be successful and bring Kemen to me. I believe in you and our men."

"Thank you, sir. We won't disappoint you." Bieito bowed his head slightly.

The vehicle fell into silence again. Bieito imagined all of the men who rode with them were thinking about the upcoming fight and, more than likely, their own families—if they had any. Not one of them was guaranteed a safe return. Hell, not even Bieito could say with one hundred percent certainty that he'd get out of the compound alive or uninjured.

The only one ensured of that was Victor, and only because Bieito had warned Samuel that if anything happened to Victor, he would take it out of Samuel's hide. The man had reassured him he'd die before he allowed that. Bieito had told him he'd better be dead or Bieito would kill him.

They hit the I-10 to head south for an hour or so. Andrew hadn't been entirely accurate in his timetable. Bieito had worked out the exact location of the Cortez estate from the coordinates the DEA and FBI had written down. They would hop off the I-10 before they hit Tucson then make their way out into the desert as close as they could to the compound without alerting anyone they were coming.

It was going to be a long night.

Chapter Fourteen

"We're here," Samuel spoke from the front seat.

Bieito opened his eyes and took a deep breath. At some point during the ride, Victor had taken Bieito's hand in his, hiding them under the jacket Victor had brought with him. A quick squeeze then Victor let go before Bieito climbed out. His men gathered around and Bieito looked each one of them in the eye. He waited until they nodded before moving on.

"All right, gentlemen," he said softly after he'd tugged his balaclava down to cover his face. "Remember. Quiet and quick. We need to be in and out before the alarm gets sounded, but if not, you shoot to kill. Once Larenz is in my custody, we leave. Most of you will head to the border and cross as best you can. Dump the weapons when you're able."

"Yes, boss," Valdez muttered.

He turned to look at Victor, who gave him one nod. "All right. Let's move out. Be careful. We have about a mile before we reach the outer edge of the compound land. We'll be following the trail that starts just beyond the small rise there." He motioned to their left. "Get out your night vision goggles."

The cartel had spent a lot of money on them, and Bieito was glad Victor had approved the expense. It would help them move through the night without alerting anyone by using flashlights. Any kind of light could be seen at far distances in the desert, especially when there weren't any mountains or trees to block it.

He gestured for Tomas, one of the men who had been with them the longest, to take point. Bieito watched the rest follow behind him, making sure there was enough space between them that an attack wouldn't take them all out at once. Bieito glanced at Victor one last time before taking his place at the end of the line. It was his job to make sure no one circled around and snuck up on them from behind. Also, he liked having everyone else in front of him where he could see them.

Trust no one was a motto his father had drilled into him from an early age. Anyone would turn on him if given the right incentive. Hell, he'd seen it a lot during his career with all the government officials and law enforcement people he'd corrupted and bribed. He'd run into very few people who wouldn't compromise their integrity, and those earned his respect. So he'd keep an eye on the men he was with and hope none of them had received a better offer.

They trooped through the sand and brush as quietly as they could, though if anyone was paying attention, they'd know something moved in the desert. All the creatures that called it home fell silent as the men went by. Bieito checked his watch. They were making good time.

"God, please look kindly on us and make sure the DEA isn't watching tonight," he muttered, sending the prayer up into the night air.

To be honest, it was his worst fear. He wasn't worried about the Cortez men. His own would be more than capable of handling them. If the DEA was around, it would make getting Kemen out of the area much more difficult. Also, sneaking Victor out of the country would be almost impossible. They'd been extremely lucky no one had noticed their plane landing under the cover of darkness two nights before.

While he might have been able to convince members of the Mexican forces to let Victor go, Bieito doubted it would work with the Americans. They took their 'war on drugs' seriously, though Bieito believed they went about it the wrong way. As long as there was a demand for the product, there would be people providing it. If they worked to do something about fixing the problem at the source—the addict—then Bieito figured demand would disappear.

He could admit to himself there were a few times when he wished that would happen and he'd be out of a job. Shaking his head, he pushed those thoughts away. It wasn't the time or the place to think that. He had to focus on his job, which was to rescue Victor's son and get him back to Mexico safely without involving the American authorities.

When he came back to the present, he noticed the men were gathered in front of him, crouched to peer over a low ridge. He joined Valdez, who motioned to the short rock barrier marking the perimeter of the Cortez land.

"I knew it was there. All the information we have on it is that it's not wired. There are no cameras out in this area," Bieito told them, keeping his voice low. "All they have are guards who walked the fence. In fact, one should be coming by in the next couple of minutes."

Tomas didn't wait for Bieito to say anything. He slipped over the ridge, fading into the darkness. According to their plans, Tomas would lie in wait for the guard then take him out as he went by. One of the men would take the guard's place, walking his beat while the other four went along to meet up and take out each guard as they came upon them.

Once the first guy was down, Bieito and his four would go over the fence and head right to the three central buildings. As far as Bieito could find out, they didn't use dogs, so at least they didn't have to worry about them.

A flicker of light showed up to their right and Bieito motioned for them all to duck. He kept his head just above the ridgeline so he could watch the man's approach. He didn't know where Tomas had settled and didn't care, as long as he got the job done. The man drew closer then the faint sound of a struggle drifted over to them.

Staying still, Bieito scanned the desert in both directions to make sure the sound hadn't alerted anyone they might not have seen. There didn't seem to be anyone around, so he gestured for the rest to stand and move toward the fence. At the same time, a low whistle signaled Tomas had taken care of business.

Once they were gathered on the other side, he motioned for Valdez to take off with his group. Bieito crooked his finger at his men and took off toward the main part of the compound. He'd chosen this time of night because he thought it was unlikely anyone except the guards would be out, and it was proving right.

Bieito didn't run into anyone or hear anything to indicate there were people who were awake. He pressed up against the wall of the first building, close to the door. After reaching for the doorknob, he double-checked to make sure everyone was in position before he slowly turned it. It wasn't locked, so entry was going to be far easier than expected.

He'd chosen Tomas to be the first one in. As he eased the door wider, Tomas slipped through. Bieito waited until he heard a faint knock on the wall then he slid into the darkness. Tomas crouched by a large crate, facing away from Bieito, but he motioned behind his back to tell Bieito where to go.

The last guy in shut the door then they proceeded to work their way through the building, checking each room and going up to the second floor as well. There was nothing but crates and a lab where Cortez's people must have broken down the different shipments and repackaged them.

When they cleared the building, not having found Kemen or any people at all, Bieito left Marcus behind to keep an eye on it along with watching their backs while they went on to the next one. The second search went much like the first, and Bieito left Philip at that door.

"Okay, gentlemen. More than likely, Larenz is in this one and there will be men guarding him," Bieito informed the final two men. "We'll have to move as quietly as possible and as quickly as we can to get him out before they figure out we're here. Once we have Larenz, we'll head out, picking up the others as we go. Valdez and his unit should be done by the time we're ready to get the hell out."

Josè and Tomas nodded. Again Tomas was the first in, and when the faint knock came to let Bieito know it was clear to come in, there was also another tap, announcing Tomas had eyes on one hostile.

"All right. Quiet and careful," Bieito whispered as he motioned for Josè to go on in.

After all three of them were inside, Tomas eased from shadow to shadow across the empty warehouse to where a young man sat, staring at his cell phone. There wasn't any warning before Tomas yanked him off the chair then dragged him into the darkness.

Scraping sounded from where they'd disappeared then stopped. Tomas stepped out into Bieito's vision and nodded. Bieito gestured for Josè to go to the left while he went right. He discovered another man sleeping in a back room then rendered him unconscious. Bieito tied and gagged him before moving on.

After making a circuit of the first floor, they met up at the base of the stairs. Tomas headed up first, Josè second and Bieito brought up the rear. He kept one ear peeled for the sound of doors opening. The radio on his hip buzzed—Valdez signaling his part of the mission was complete.

At the top of the stairs, Tomas went in one direction and Josè the other down the hallway. Bieito stayed where he was, poised to go either way. He heard a shoe rub on the metal under his feet and he glanced to see Tomas headed back toward him. So that meant Kemen was in one of the rooms Josè was looking through.

The door at the end of the hall slammed against the wall and a man tumbled out, yelling as he did. Bieito and Tomas dropped to the floor, letting the bullets fly over top of them. Josè took their assailant out before he could readjust his aim.

Before the body even hit the ground, Bieito was up and moving. He dashed into the room, jerking off his goggles as he did so. Feeling around for the light switch, he managed to find it then flipped it on.

"Who the fuck are you?"

He couldn't help but smile because right at that moment, Kemen sounded exactly like Victor. "I'm here to rescue you."

Kemen eyed him from where he sat, tied to a chair. He looked like Cortez's men had worked him over a bit, and Bieito knew Victor wasn't going to like that. One more mark would be added to the column of why Victor was going to destroy Cortez and his cartel.

"Are you police or some kind of law enforcement?" Kemen seemed rather suspicious. Not that Bieito could blame him.

"No. But we're the good guys," he told him as he approached then crouched to start cutting through the ropes.

Kemen snarled. "Why should I believe you? Something tells me you're just as bad as the men who kidnapped me."

Bieito tilted his head for a second while he thought. "I suppose we are, but what makes us different is we aren't here to kill you."

"Not yet anyway," Kemen muttered.

Rising up onto his knees, Bieito leaned in to whisper, "Not ever. You have no idea just how special you are."

Before Kemen could reply, he cut through the last of Kemen's bindings then stood to hold his hand.

"Can you walk?"

Knocking his hand aside, Kemen pushed to his feet. "I'm tired of being dragged here and there without anyone telling me anything, except to ask me what I know about my father. I demand you tell me where you're taking me."

Tomas started to step in, lifting his hand to hit Kemen for talking to Bieito that way. Bieito caught the man's arm, shaking him slightly.

"Remember what Señor Delarosa said. If you touch him, you will suffer," Bieito warned Tomas.

"Yes, boss." Tomas turned around. "We should be going. Those shots could have alerted people in the other buildings."

Bieito nodded. "Right. Tomas, you and Josè head out. I'll bring Larenz with me."

Without waiting to hear what else Kemen had to say, Bieito gripped the younger man's arm before pulling him after him. "If you need help, say something. I'll carry you if I have to, but you aren't being left behind."

"Delarosa? How the fuck did I end up in the middle of some kind of dispute between drug cartels?" Kemen tried to break Bieito's hold, but it was obvious he was in more pain then he'd let on.

Slowing down a little, Bieito had Kemen go in front of him as they were heading down the stairs. Gunfire sounded outside, causing all of them to pause just inside the exit. Bieito yanked his radio from his pocket, pushing on the Call button.

"Status," he barked into it.

"There are twenty hostiles out here, boss," Valdez reported immediately. "We can blow a hole through them to get you headed back to the vehicles, but you're going to have to double time it."

He glanced over at Kemen, who grimaced. "All right. I'm sure by now Samuel and Señor Delarosa have moved, so we're heading right out the front gates, gentlemen. Can you lay down suppressive fire while we make a run for it?"

"Yes, we can. Actually, we're by the front gates now, rigging them to blow. Give us another two minutes before you come out though," Valdez advised.

"Signal when we can go," Bieito ordered then stuffed the radio into his pocket. He stripped off his vest, tossing it to Kemen. "Here. Put this on."

Kemen stared at him. "Why would you give me your protection?"

"We don't want you dead," Bieito told him softly, making sure Tomas and Josè were far enough away that they couldn't hear him. "I said it before and I'll say it again. You're important."

"Does this have anything to do with those men asking me about my father and Delarosa?" A horrified look crossed Kemen's face. "Is Victor Delarosa my father?"

Bieito sighed. "That's a conversation you'll have to discuss with him. I'm only here to retrieve you and get you across the border back into Mexico. Once there, you will have your answers."

Kemen put on the vest before resting his hand on Bieito's arm. "Is my mother all right?"

Chapter Fifteen

"When I last saw her, yes." That was all he was going to say about that. A large explosion rocked the area then his radio buzzed. "Tomas, you go first. Josè next. Larenz, you stay between Josè and me. We'll do our best to protect you, but if one of us goes down, you just keep running. There's another group of my men waiting for us at the gates, plus our vehicles will be waiting as well."

Once they were arranged the way Bieito wanted, he motioned for Tomas to head out. The front man kicked the door open and they ran. Bieito kept his head up, trying to pick off shooters, but hoping as well that one of his own men didn't take advantage of the situation and kill him to try and take his place. *Ah…the joys of not trusting the people I work with.*

Covering fire came from just ahead of them, along with shots from both sides. They were running a gauntlet, and Bieito could only pray they were moving fast enough so that no one would get lucky.

"Keep going," he shouted when Tomas hesitated at the blown gate. Bieito gestured for the rest of the unit to join them as they went through the cloud of dirt and debris to where the two SUVs idled.

He'd been right, knowing Victor would've decided leaving the compound this way would be the fastest and easiest exit. The back door of the second SUV flew open and Bieito practically tossed Kemen into it. He dove in after him while Tomas jumped into the passenger seat. The rest loaded into the front vehicle.

"Valdez said the explosives are set to go off in five minutes. It should give us enough time to get farther away," Tomas informed Bieito, who struggled to straighten up.

"Get the fuck out of here, Samuel," he demanded.

"Yes, boss." Samuel threw the vehicle into Drive, slinging gravel as he followed the other SUV down the faint trail.

Bieito shifted and shoved Kemen around until they were both sitting on the seat. Then he noticed the tension and silence filling the air. He tore his mask off, letting it drop to the floor while he studied the two Delarosas, who stared at each other.

"You're my fucking father," Kemen muttered.

Victor nodded. "Hello, Kemen. I'm Victor Delarosa and yes, I'm your father."

Biting back a chuckle, Bieito turned his head away for a second. *That announcement is rather Star Wars-like.* He heard a grunt and twisted around to see Kemen throwing a punch at Victor. He assumed the noise he'd heard was Victor reacting to the first hit.

Bieito wrapped his hand around Kemen's arm. "No hitting him. At least not while we're fleeing for our lives. Once we're home, you two can fight and yell and do whatever you want. We don't have time for this."

Victor shot him a disgruntled look, but Bieito didn't care. It wasn't often he spoke to Victor like that in front of anyone, yet he was right. There wasn't enough room for them to go at each other physically, plus Kemen was injured.

"We'll need to have the doctor look him over once we get back," he told Victor.

"Cortez hurt you?" Victor started to touch Kemen but let his hand drop when Kemen jerked out of reach.

"Of course he fucking hurt me. His men beat the shit out of me because I wouldn't tell them anything about my father. I kept explaining I had no idea who my father was, but they didn't believe me." Kemen waved a hand shakily at Victor. "It makes sense now. They probably thought I was lying to protect you."

"I'll kill him," Victor muttered.

Kemen inhaled sharply as Samuel skidded the truck off the driveway onto the road, which caused Kemen to land hard against Bieito.

"Here. Let's get this off you," Bieito suggested. "I have food and water for you as well. I'm pretty sure they didn't feed you."

He could tell Kemen wanted to refuse—from general principle—but his hunger and thirst would override his anger and pride. Bieito tossed the vest over the seat into the back before digging through one of the duffels. He got out water, a couple of protein bars and a bottle of ibuprofen.

After handing two of the items to Kemen, he opened the ibuprofen then shook out two pills. "Here. It'll help dull the pain a little until we can get a doctor to look you over."

Kemen shook his head. "I don't want drugs."

"It's over the counter medicine, Larenz. Nothing more sinister than that." He dropped them into Kemen's hand. "I wouldn't try to drug you."

He took them then looked over to where Victor sat quietly with a thoughtful expression on his face. "Why should I trust you?"

"You shouldn't," Victor admitted, causing Bieito to roll his eyes at the honesty. "All you know about me is I'm a drug kingpin and your absentee father. There's no foundation between us to make you believe I mean you no harm."

Kemen snorted. "Right. So as soon as you can, you need to drop me off at the nearest police station."

"Why would we do that?" Bieito asked from where he'd wedged himself into the corner of the back seat, sipping on his own bottle of water.

Giving him a look that said he clearly thought Bieito was mentally deficient, Kemen said, "So I can report my kidnapping and figure out how to get home."

"You do realize you have no passport, no proof that you really were kidnapped. The compound you were just at is pretty much a pile of rubble now, and all law enforcement will be heading in that direction," Bieito pointed out. "If they do have time to deal with you, you'll be labeled an illegal. They'll toss you into a cell then deport you back to Mexico."

"I'll have them call my mother. She'll explain the situation." Kemen sounded confident about his mother's ability to sway officials.

Bieito pursed his lips, but Victor spoke up before he could speak.

"Your mother is at my compound. I kept her there, so she couldn't tell her lover I was coming after you," Victor explained.

"Her lover? Mitchell?" Kemen shrugged. "Why would that matter? Mitchell's so coked out, most of the time he doesn't remember his own name."

"Seems like he owed the Cortez cartel quite a bit of money because of his habit. A little pillow talk from your mother, telling him that you were my son, was all he needed to pay back his debt." Victor rubbed his palms over his pants in a rather nervous gesture. "Your mother arrived at my compound to tell me about your kidnapping in a vehicle owned by Cortez."

Bieito was prepared this time when Kemen went for Victor. He caught the younger man around the waist then shifted until he was sitting between the two Delarosas. Poking his finger into Kemen's chest, he snarled.

"Not fucking now. I told you wait until we get home then you can have as big a knock-down drag-out fight as you want and I won't stop either of you." He pinched the bridge of his nose. "There are days when I'm pretty sure I'm too fucking old for this shit anymore," he muttered.

Victor glanced around him at Kemen. "Perez is right. We'll call a truce until we are back home safely. Once we've achieved that, you and I will talk about everything."

"And my mother," Kemen said.

"You will get to hear her side of the story," Victor conceded. He settled into Bieito's side, the movement and position hidden by the darkness. "Rest as best you can. We should be getting to the airport in about three hours."

Bieito could tell Kemen wanted to say something else, but a yawn interrupted him.

Grabbing a jacket from the back, he held it out to Kemen. "You can either put this on or use it as a pillow. I'll wake you up when we get there."

Kemen took it from him then sighed. "Thank you. I know you're only doing what you were ordered to do, but I do appreciate you risking your life to save me."

"You're welcome. Now shut up and go to sleep." Bieito really wanted to shut his own eyes and come down from the adrenaline high, but he figured that wasn't going to happen any time soon.

When it became obvious Kemen had done exactly what Bieito had told him to do, Bieito turned to Victor and said softly, "You're going to have to fight an uphill battle with this one."

Victor nodded. "Yes, but I can't really be insulted, can I? I haven't been in his life except as a guardian angel from afar. He only knows what he's read about me, and none of that is good."

Bieito twisted a little to rest his hand on Victor's thigh. He figured Victor could use the reassurance right then. Not that he'd ever seen the man lack in self-confidence, but it must be hard to have your only son reject you the instant he saw you.

"Plus, he'll take his mother's side in everything because she was the one who raised and loved him," Victor pointed out.

"Even if she was the one who sold him out in the end," Bieito murmured.

"Right. None of us want to believe our parents would do something like that, though some of us know what it's like to be seen as merely an object in their eyes, not a person to be treasured."

He squeezed Victor's knee, knowing he was thinking about his own father. "At least you chose to allow Kemen to live on his own terms, not like your father, who forced you back to the compound and to the cartel."

"I could've run," Victor said, but they both knew that wasn't true.

"If you had, he would've hunted you down and either dragged you back or killed you where he found you." Bieito shook his head. "Your father had no emotional attachment to you or Pablo."

"Which was why it was easy for him to let our mother take Pablo." Victor covered Bieito's hand with his. "I think the one thing that comforted me the most while growing up is that I knew how much it hurt my mother to leave me behind. I remember her sobbing and hugging me, whispering how sorry she was. Pablo has often said she spoke to him about me, and he told me about the nights he'd heard her crying in her room when he was supposed to be asleep."

Bieito hummed softly for a second. "I know. My mom used to say your mother was the strongest woman she knew. She didn't think she'd be able to give me up just to save her other child."

Victor snorted. "Your mother would've taken you and your siblings—if you'd had any—without hesitation. She wasn't afraid of your father, unlike the rest of the reasonably intelligent people who dealt with him."

Turning his head so their lips were inches apart, Bieito whispered, "My mom loved you. She considered you a second son, and the way your father treated you made her angry. If my father hadn't stopped her, she would've told your father off so many times. I think my father didn't want to have to punish her, which was what would've happened if she'd done that."

Victor pressed a quick kiss on Bieito's mouth before easing farther away. "You're right." Exhaling sharply, he shot a look over Bieito's shoulder at his sleeping son. "What do I do with him? If he doesn't accept me and wants to leave, how do I stop him?"

"You don't. You let him go then do what you've been doing. Put a guard on him, but one that doesn't intrude on his life. All you can do is keep an eye on him and hope he stays safe." Bieito shrugged. "He would've been fine if his mother hadn't picked the wrong boyfriend to impress."

"Yes. We're going to have to deal with him at some point," Victor mused.

Bieito knew that was going to come up, and he'd already put a plan into action. "Don't worry. Mitchell won't ever think to even his debts by using your son again."

Victor chuckled. "I should've known you already took care of that."

"It's my job to anticipate things you'll want done," he confessed then yawned.

"You should try to rest as well. We still have a while before we get to the airstrip. I'm pretty sure we're out of trouble at the moment. Samuel and Tomas will keep an eye out for now."

As much as Bieito wanted to say he was fine, it had to be obvious he was exhausted. He settled into the seat, letting his head drop back. Before he let sleep grab him, he told Victor, "Have Tomas call the pilot and make sure the plane's ready for us."

"I will," Victor promised.

He took a quick peek at Kemen to make sure he was still sleeping then shut his eyes. The kid was safe now. Whatever happened next would work itself out.

Chapter Sixteen

"What the fuck happened?" Penn yelled, forcing Snap to hold the phone away from his ear. "When I went to bed last night, everything was fine. Then I'm awakened in the middle of the night by that fucking FBI guy and told that the Cortez compound has been blown to high heaven. Where were you two?"

"Umm...we were in our hotel room in Phoenix," Snap informed him and Dalton cringed next to him. "We'd made plans to meet up with the local DEA guys and go to check the area out the next morning. How were we supposed to know someone was going blow it up?"

Penn huffed his annoyance. "God, I hate when you're being logical. Are you at least going to look the place over now?"

"Yes. We're on our way there now," Snap said. "From the first update we got, there were quite a few dead, but so far, they seem to be known members of the Cortez cartel. There hasn't been any kind of clue as to who did it and why."

"We know who fucking did it. We just have to figure out how the fuck he got into the country and why the fuck he's taking out Cortez's men," Penn muttered. "Keep me in the loop, Jefferson. This is a major problem. The cartels have never brought their wars onto American soil before. This could be what we're looking for to go after Delarosa."

Snap nodded then said, "Yes, sir. I'll call you after we've gotten a look at the compound."

Penn ended the call and Snap stuffed his phone into the pocket of his jacket. He shared an exasperated look with Dalton, who was driving.

"Does he really believe Victor Delarosa crossed the border to do this?" Dalton shook his head.

"No. He thinks it was Perez, since we heard that rumor he'd been sighted in Phoenix a day or two before. If it was Perez, you know he was acting on Delarosa's orders." Snap rubbed his hand over his bald head. "But what the hell brought this attack on? Cortez and Delarosa have been going after each other for decades, but never like this and never in the States."

Dalton shrugged. "I don't know. Maybe if we examine the pictures of people coming and going from the compound in the days leading up to this, we'll discover something. I don't think Cortez has left Mexico in years, so it can't be him they were after."

Snap grunted when he saw the car in front of them turn off the paved road onto a dirt trail. "I guess we'll find out. It might be the first move in Delarosa trying to corner the market in shipping drugs into the States. Cortez is his only real competition."

His partner gripped the steering wheel of their vehicle tight as they bounced through ruts and holes. "I can't believe no one was out here watching last night. It must have been like shooting fish in a barrel for Perez. He didn't have to worry about law enforcement interfering."

"Did he know that though, or was he just rolling the dice that we wouldn't be around?" Snap slapped his hand against his thigh. "There are too many questions involved in this and I don't like it."

"I don't either," Dalton muttered.

They pulled to a stop in front of a ruined gate. It was obvious some kind of explosion had happened just from the debris of rock, dirt and concrete lying around. They climbed out to get a closer look. Snap realized it was going to be a long day.

* * * *

Victor leaned against the edge of his desk, watching as Kemen and Esperanza reunited. She gushed over him while shooting daggers at Victor, who merely raised an eyebrow back at her. She wasn't as immaculately dressed as she had been when she'd arrived. He'd given Romero the orders to make sure Esperanza was fed three times a day, but she wasn't allowed any other contact with the employees.

He wasn't going to let her abuse them because she was pissed at him. They worked for him and he believed in treating them with respect. Well, until they gave him a reason not to. It was far different than how his father had treated them, which was why he did it.

"Oh, my poor baby. Are you all right?" Esperanza touched the bruise under Kemen's eye. "I was so scared."

"I'm fine, Mom. Señor Delarosa had his personal physician check me out." Kemen glanced at him, obviously reluctant to admit Victor had done anything nice for him.

She sniffed. "Of course he did. He's your father and it's his fault you were taken in the first place."

Victor started to straighten, but Bieito, who'd been standing quietly in the corner of the room, spoke first. "I'm sorry, Señora Larenz. That's not true. If your boyfriend hadn't told Cortez who Kemen was, he would've never been kidnapped. How would Mitchell have found out about Kemen's father if you hadn't said anything to him?"

Esperanza turned her back on Bieito. "You don't get to speak without being given permission. You're just an employee. Stay silent."

Bieito blinked at her tone and Victor stood. He walked over to her. After grabbing her wrist, he tugged her close to him, leaning into her personal space so all she could focus on was his face. He ignored Kemen's protest or the little squeak of fear Esperanza gave.

"I suggest you never take that tone with Perez again. He might work for me, but he is far more than just an employee. He is the most trusted member of my staff, plus he is the one who went in and rescued Kemen, at great risk to his own life," Victor snapped. "You might be the mother of my child, Esperanza, but you are *not* a valued member of my household."

He tightened his grip then let her go. Kemen didn't rush to her side, though he did send a nasty frown in Victor's direction. She held her hand close to her chest and dropped to the couch behind her.

"Besides, what Perez said was true. No one—except for you and I—knew who Kemen's father was. I never shared that information with anyone. Suddenly, Kemen is kidnapped by my archrival, and the only new person in the equation is Mitchell. You do realize I've known about his drug habit since you started dating him? I should've dealt with him at the very beginning, but I chose to let him stay around." Victor shook his head. "I should've gone with my instincts on that one."

"We all make mistakes," Bieito said, sharing a brief smile with him.

"True." Victor returned to his desk but didn't sit. "Kemen, my doctor says you're fine, aside from bruising. No broken bones or anything like that. I would normally let you go back to your life, but unfortunately, I'm going to have to ask you to stay here on the compound for a little while longer."

"I can't do that. I have a life to go back to," Esperanza informed him.

Victor eyed her. "I'm asking Kemen to stay here. You, my dear, are free to leave. Also, you will be vacating the house I bought for you within the month. You'll receive one thousand dollars a month from me from now on, but that is it. I won't be supporting you and your lovers anymore."

"A thousand?" Her shriek caused all three of them to wince. "I can't live off a thousand a month. And you can't make me move. That house is mine."

"Yes, Señor Delarosa can make you move. I went over the contract and he owns the house outright. Your name doesn't appear on the ownership papers. There's no lease, either." Bieito shuffled through a file he'd been holding. After removing a paper, he handed it to Kemen. "You're more knowledgeable about things like this, I'm sure. Here is the agreement between your parents when your father returned home and your mother refused to come with him."

Kemen took it then read it over. Victor watched an interesting expression come over his face. He couldn't tell what his son was thinking and he was usually quite adept at reading people.

He was so caught up in Kemen, he missed Esperanza launching herself from the couch to fly at him. The sound of her hitting him rang through the room then she was spewing curses as Bieito dragged her away from Victor.

"Mother," Kemen gasped. "Get a hold of yourself."

"You don't get to treat me like trash. You can't just throw me out on the street. What about your son? Where is he going to live?" Esperanza struggled against Bieito's hold, but Victor knew she wouldn't be able to break free.

Kemen opened his mouth and closed it, seemingly unsure how to react to the way his mother was acting. Victor shook his head.

"I'm not throwing Kemen out on the street. I will continue to pay for his education and buy a house for him. Though there will be the stipulation that you will not be allowed to live there with him. You've taken advantage of my good nature long enough, Esperanza."

"Your good nature? Does a drug lord have one of those?" Kemen interjected.

Bieito laughed from where he stood, hand on Esperanza's shoulder to keep her from going after Victor again. "He has a point."

"Shut up, Perez." He turned back to Kemen. "I want you to stay here for as long as it takes to clean up this mess. Once Cortez has been taken out, you can return to your life and I'll never grace your doorstep again unless you want me to."

Kemen frowned as he stared at Victor then faced his mother. "Did you really take his money but refuse to let him see me?"

Her eyes filled with tears and her bottom lip trembled. "Kemen, *el nino*. I love you. I was only thinking about you. Do you seriously want it known Victor Delarosa is your father? You'd be looking over your shoulder the rest of your life."

"She's right," Victor agreed. "I can't help that, but what I can promise is there will be people watching you the entire time."

Kemen cringed. "I'm not sure I want that."

Bieito huffed. "Your guards would be there to protect you if need be. I guarantee that for the most part, you'll never know they're around. I'll have trained them, and as Señor Delarosa can tell you, I'm the best."

"He is. I'm still alive, aren't I?" Victor smirked a little when Bieito rolled his eyes.

"You're not forcing me to stay here though, are you?" Kemen pursed his lips and a little wrinkle appeared on his forehead.

Victor closed his eyes and took a deep breath before he said, "No, I'm not going to force you to stay here. I'm asking that you stay until I can deal with the Cortez problem. Within the next month, it should be fixed and you'll be safe to go back to the university."

Kemen hummed then asked, "Can I have the rest of the day to think about it? I'm not entirely sure how I feel about being protected by the head of a cartel."

That was a fair request. "Yes. You can give me your answer tomorrow. I have to be honest though, if you decide to leave here, I'll probably send some men with you. Again, only until the situation has been dealt with."

"And that is fair as well," Kemen admitted.

"What about me?" Esperanza inquired, tugging against Bieito's hand. "Are you going to toss me to the wolves?"

Victor didn't want to say it in front of Kemen, but he couldn't get away with showing mercy to her. "Yes, I am. You did this to yourself, my dear. You came here in a vehicle owned by the Cortez cartel. That tells me you have more of a connection to them than you admit to, and I'm not going to allow that. You should be happy I don't have you killed for betraying Kemen and me like you did."

She gulped as though suddenly realizing just how lucky she was that Bieito hadn't removed her from the study to end her life. It was the only leniency Victor was willing to show her, and it was simply because she was Kemen's mother.

"I should be happy?" Obviously, she couldn't stay quiet though. "I gave birth to your son and I should be happy you don't have me murdered? You're a bastard, Victor."

He couldn't argue with that. "You're not telling me anything I don't know, Esperanza. You knew that from when we met, but I did ask you to come with me when I came back home. You chose to stay in Mexico City, raising Kemen on your own, using my money."

"There were a lot of nannies," Kemen commented.

Victor kept his mouth shut on that. He wasn't going to badmouth Esperanza anymore in front of Kemen. The young man would make up his own mind about his mother and continue to love her anyway.

Loving someone meant seeing their faults, accepting them and keeping them in your heart. It was how he loved Bieito and how Bieito cared for him as well.

"We'll meet in the morning for breakfast and you can give me your answer then. You can say goodbye to your mother now. She'll be leaving within the hour." He gestured for Bieito to follow him. "Esperanza, I'll be sending Romero to escort you out. Don't cause trouble, or Perez will be the one who takes you to your car."

"I'll make sure she doesn't, sir," Kemen promised as Victor left.

He led the way into the small dining room where a light meal had been set for them. Victor asked one of the maids to take some food into his study for Kemen and Esperanza. Once that was done, he took a seat next to Bieito then filled his plate.

"What do you think he'll decide?" He kept his voice low.

Bieito took a bite then swallowed before he said, "I think Kemen is a smart guy. He'll work out the best plan for him to stay alive is to remain here until we destroy Cortez. And while he might not be happy about it, he'll accept the guards you'll put on him."

Victor began eating while running through his options. When he finished and his plate was empty, he picked up his coffee mug then leaned back in his chair. "Who do you suggest we put on Kemen?"

"Tomas and Valdez. I trained both of them, and they are the best we have, since I can't go." Bieito pushed his plate away before taking his cup. He assumed the same position as Victor. "I trust them. It's up to you whether you tell them Kemen is your son or not. You can simply say he's someone you need under surveillance and to make sure nothing happens to him."

"I'll have to mull that over. I have time." He ran his finger over the rim of his mug. "We need to decide how we're going to take Cortez down for what he did to Kemen. Also, where did you put all the money you gathered for the ransom?"

"It's in the vault until I have the time to return it to the various establishments I took it from." Bieito checked his watch. "We have the rest of the evening to organize the plan, though I believe on just hitting every known Cortez associate. Once they're taken out, we go after the main group at Cortez's compound. He won't have enough people left to defend the area."

Victor thought it sounded like a good idea. "All right. We'll go to your office for now. Once that's solidified, we can bring in the others as we need them."

Bieito stood. "I'll tell Maria to bring us lots of coffee. I have all the schematics for Cortez's compound, plus an extensive list of the men who work for him."

"I'm not surprised you have that, but why do you have it?" Victor joined him as they walked out of the room.

"I have it because I knew you'd reach this decision at some point and I wanted to be ready." Bieito winked at him while holding open the door to his office. "I'm prepared for all occasions."

"Yes, you are." Victor waited until the door was shut behind them before he pushed Bieito back against it. "I think we need to let off a little energy then we can get started."

Bieito leaned down to crush their lips together and Victor hummed, loving the way Bieito tasted.

Bieito began to unbutton Victor's pants while placing biting kisses along his jaw. It was going to be quick and dirty. Once he got Victor's belt and zipper undone, he shoved them down to the man's knees.

"Turn around. I'm fucking you right now. You can take me later when we're in your bed," he whispered in Victor's ear. "I don't have any lube, so it's going to hurt a little."

Victor tilted his ass up while resting his head on the wall. "You know I don't care about that. Just fuck me, Bieito. I've wanted this since you jumped into the SUV after saving Kemen."

"All that excitement and danger turns you on," he murmured, fumbling with his own clothes, growling in frustration when he couldn't get his zipper down. He laid his forehead between Victor's shoulder blades then took a deep breath to calm himself. As much as he wanted to be inside Victor, he needed to slow down a little or else he'd end up hurting him.

"Just breathe," Victor murmured, reaching back to pat Bieito's hip.

When he thought he could control himself, he went back to getting his pants open. Bieito rubbed his cock over Victor's ass then pushed his fingers into Victor's mouth.

"Suck."

Victor did so without protesting Bieito's abrupt order. He got Bieito's fingers as wet as he could before Bieito removed them to push them against Victor's hole. Victor rocked back and they both moaned when he sank in.

"Don't take forever," Victor begged.

Bieito didn't. A few strokes in and out then he spat into the palm of his hand. After coating his cock, he settled between Victor's legs before slowly breaching his hole. He didn't stop until he was pressed tight against Victor's back.

Slipping his arm around Victor's waist, he kissed the nape of Victor's neck. "Are you all right?" he asked, not willing to move until Victor told him it was okay.

Victor took a deep breath and Bieito could feel him relax then tighten around him. "You can fuck me," Victor told him.

"Thank God," he muttered as he began to stroke in and out.

Victor braced his hands on the wall, rocking back into each thrust. Their breaths came in pants with low grunts mixed in. Bieito sped up, his smooth rhythm disappearing the longer he fucked Victor. The pressure built behind his balls and they drew close to his body.

Bieito ached with the need to come, but he didn't want to until Victor had. So he slid down to take Victor's shaft in hand. He pumped in time with his own thrusts.

"Oh God, Bieito," Victor said as he let his head drop back onto Bieito's shoulder. "I love the touch of your hand."

"I love how tight your ass is and how it fits my cock like a glove," he confessed, slamming into Victor.

"Fuck," Victor shouted and came, spilling his seed all over Bieito's hand.

The way his inner channel massaged Bieito's length drew Bieito's climax from him as well. They rocked together for a few more moments until Bieito was pretty sure every last drop had been drained from him.

His legs threatened to collapse under him, and he leaned into Victor, waiting for the strength to return to them. When he was sure he could move, he slid out to shuffle over to his desk where he pulled out some tissues to wipe himself off. After refastening his pants, he grabbed more tissues then went back to where Victor stood.

He bit Victor's butt cheek before cleaning him. Victor glared at him as he rearranged his clothes, but Bieito chuckled.

"Hey, you have a nice ass. I couldn't resist," he said.

"Fuck you." Victor went to sit on the chair closest to Bieito's desk.

"You'll get to do that later on," Bieito reminded him as he unlocked the door before going to a cabinet where he stored the information he'd gathered on Cortez. It was going to be a long night, but at least he had something to look forward to after they'd finished their plans.

Chapter Seventeen

"All hell is breaking lose in Mexico," Snap told Mac as they stood out in Mac's backyard.

Mac frowned. "What's happened now? We hadn't received the update yet before I left today."

Snap looked back over his shoulder to where Ken and Tanner were seated at the kitchen island counter, talking while Tanner finished the last minute touches to their dinner. After taking a sip of his beer, Snap shook his head slowly.

"Delarosa is taking Cortez apart. Every day more bodies turn up. The only good thing is none of them are innocents. There hasn't been any collateral damage yet." He wiggled his hand back and forth. "It all started when he hit the Cortez compound in Arizona. Something pissed Delarosa off and he decided Cortez needed to be destroyed."

"Have you figured out why he sent Perez all the way up here to start his war?" Mac sighed. "It doesn't make sense. Victor's not impulsive or stupid. He knows that doing this will ensure the authorities come after him as well. They can't afford to allow him to continue this, even if he's only killing bad guys."

Snap looked back at their men again then met Mac's concerned gaze. "Of course he knows that, but he doesn't care. We're still going through all the pictures our agents took of people coming and going from the Cortez place before it blew up. We haven't found any person who might be a reason for him to lose his mind like this."

"Fuck," Mac cursed before taking a swig from his bottle.

"Have you told Tanner any of this?" Snap hadn't said anything to Ken, having a feeling Ken wouldn't care about it. He had no familial connection to Victor, so he wouldn't worry about the man.

Mac grimaced. "Not all the details. He's seen it on the news and I know he's worried about Victor and Perez. They haven't contacted him in a week or so."

He rubbed his chin. "He's exterminating the men who work for Cortez. To be honest, everyone who's been monitoring this says he's going after Cortez once all the foot soldiers are gone."

"Do you think Cortez will try a preemptive strike against Delarosa? Try to take him out before he has no army left?" Mac inquired before emptying his drink.

"It's a possibility, but so far, Cortez just seems to be hunkering down at his personal compound down in the south of Mexico. No one's seen him in over six months. The rumor in the law enforcement circles is Cortez is ill. Hell, he's been the head of the cartel for a long time. Same age as Delarosa's father would've been if he was still alive." Snap shrugged. "I wouldn't be surprised if he doesn't do anything until Delarosa comes after him on his own territory."

Mac didn't reply as they made their way back inside. Snap couldn't blame him. What could he say when more than likely his lover's brother was either going to be killed in a drug war or arrested by law enforcement? Either way, Tanner was going to lose Victor, and while they hadn't spent any time together over the years, at least Tanner had known Victor was out there in the world.

"Hey, guys, perfect timing. I just pulled dinner out of the oven." Tanner motioned for Mac to grab the basket of biscuits while he took the platter of chicken. "Were you discussing the war Victor has stared with Cortez?"

"I should've known you were on top of it," Snap commented as he sat next to Ken.

Ken glanced at him. "What's going on with Delarosa?"

"He seems to have declared war on Cortez, and from the looks of it, he means to completely wipe the Cortez cartel off the face of the earth." Mac handed him a bowl of salad.

"Have many people been killed?" Ken didn't seem concerned about Delarosa.

Snap frowned. "No innocent people have been, as far as anyone can figure out. It's as though he knows exactly who works for Cortez and he sends out hit squads to take them out. Over thirty men have died since this started."

Ken nodded but didn't ask any more questions. He started eating and the others followed his lead. Snap decided they weren't going to talk about it for the rest of the night either. He didn't want to ruin Tanner's night by discussing the possibility of his brother dying.

Eventually, the reality would hit home, but not yet, and Snap was secretly hoping Victor had figured a way out.

* * * *

Victor stared down at the phone in his hand. Was it time to reveal the truth, or should he keep up the masquerade for a while longer? He tipped his head to one side as he listened to Bieito talk to Marcus and Philip in the other room.

They'd just returned from a successful mission and Bieito was debriefing them. The list of Cortez's men was getting shorter and shorter. After Victor and Bieito had planned the entire campaign a week ago, Bieito had started it the very next day. It had been successful so far.

"Señor Delarosa?"

He glanced up to see Kemen standing in the doorway. "I told you before, Kemen. Please call me Victor. I don't expect you'll ever call me Father and that's fine."

His son dipped his head for a second then said, "Victor, may I come in?"

"Certainly." He motioned to the couch as he stood then went to join Kemen. "Was there something you needed?"

Kemen had chosen to stay at the compound like Victor had asked. He hadn't complained, especially when Bieito had shown him that he could still do most of his school courses over the Internet. Kemen had been happy to know he wasn't going to miss any of his classes.

Esperanza had driven away without looking back, and Victor didn't know if she'd contacted Kemen since. He hadn't inquired after her, knowing it wasn't his place to ask. Yet he found he was enjoying getting to know his son and wished they'd been able to spend time together while Kemen was growing up. Victor had told Kemen all about his family.

"Not really," Kemen said, flopping onto the couch. "I just thought I'd come see how you were doing. I know you've been busy with this whole war against the Cortez people."

Nodding, he replied, "Yes, though Perez has been more involved in the day-to-day business of it."

Kemen frowned and Victor sighed. "I know you don't agree with this, Kemen, but I can't allow the insult to go unpunished. If I were to let it go, they would think they could do it all the time. They might even go after your uncle, which I can't have happen either."

"Would they really go after Pablo all the way up in Texas? That seems a little out there, especially with him being a former FBI agent and his partner a Texas Ranger." Kemen didn't look convinced.

Shrugging, Victor turned the phone he still held over in his hands. "It might seem far-fetched to you, but Cortez has people all over the States who would do it."

"It's a huge risk." Kemen shifted and grimaced. "I can't see them getting away with it, simply because the American government wouldn't allow one of their citizens to be kidnapped like that."

"You might be right about it. To be honest, I would hate to have Macario come after me. He loves Pablo fiercely and I truly believe he would do anything and everything he had to do to get him back safely."

"Even break laws?"

He nodded. "Yes. Sometimes the laws can be overlooked when it comes to love. It's hard to live life in a black and white world when shades of gray dominate."

Kemen dropped his gaze to his lap. "Yeah, I get that." Then he took a deep breath before he blurted out, "Are you and Bieito lovers?"

Covering his shock, he asked, "Is that what you came to talk about?"

"No. I really did want to check on you." Kemen ran his fingers over the seams of the cushions beside him. "It just kind of spilled out. I see how he looks at you when he thinks no one is watching him. I hear how your voice changes when you talk about him, even though you never call him by his first name in front of people."

"There are reasons why, Kemen," he told him softly.

Kemen jerked his head up and down. "Yeah. I get that, but I won't say anything to anyone. Hell, you don't even have to say anything else."

He reached out to rest his hand on Kemen's knee. "Bieito and I have been lovers for over eighteen years, since shortly after he returned from college. I loved your mother at first, but when she refused to come home with me, I let go of her. Then I saw him and knew he was to be the other half of my soul. It might not be acceptable in our world for two men to love each other, but I don't give a fuck about what others think."

"Then why do you keep it a secret?"

"Because I won't risk his life and he won't risk mine. We keep it between us. As long as he knows I love him and I know he feels the same, we don't feel the need to bring it out into the open." Victor squeezed Kemen's knee. "Do you have a problem with it?"

Kemen shook his head forcefully. "No. As strange as it might sound, I have more faith in your relationship than I ever did with any of Mother's, even though hers took place out in the light of society. They always felt so fake and desperate. You and Bieito care for each other and it shows in how you protect each other."

"I'm glad you don't have a problem with it." A swell of sadness rose in him, but he tamped it down. "You do trust him to protect you as well, right?"

Chuckling, Kemen commented, "Of course I trust him. He would take a bullet for me, simply because I'm your son, just as he would for Pablo or anyone else you cared about. He's devoted to you."

Kemen's words touched Victor deep in his soul and hurt his heart as well. He knew Bieito would give up his life to keep Victor safe—whether that meant taking a bullet for him or going to jail. Yet it was coming to a point where Victor had to make a decision about his future, and it was a decision that would affect Bieito and Kemen, and he wasn't quite ready to do it.

Victor sighed. "He is, and the feeling is completely mutual." He checked his watch. "It's time for supper. Let's go see what Maria and the cook made for us."

After standing, he returned the phone to his desk drawer, locking it before following Kemen out toward the smaller dining room where they'd begun to take their meals together. He stopped by Bieito's office then looked in.

Bieito glanced up from where he stood, going over a chart with two other men. "Yes, sir?"

"Just wondering if you would be joining Kemen and me for supper?"

"I'll be there in a few minutes. We have a few last minute things to go over before Marcus and Philip go back out," Bieito informed him.

"Perfect." He inclined his head to the others. "Good job, gentlemen. There will be bonuses handed out at the end of this."

He saw a pleased look cross his men's faces, and he smiled before ducking back out to stroll over to where Kemen waited. Kemen eyed him, causing him to raise an eyebrow in question.

"Why give them a bonus?" Kemen took his usual seat to Victor's left.

"Because it gives them more of an incentive to get the job done and to do it right. They know they'll get money for it, but they also know they'll be punished if they fail." Victor shrugged. "I prefer to offer them a carrot rather than a whip."

Kemen fell silent while they got their plates ready. They were just beginning to eat when Bieito wandered into the room, talking on his phone. He ended the call before taking the spot to Victor's right.

"Sorry about that," he said, holding up his phone then stuffing it into his pocket. "Needed to get an update on how the Mexican army is dealing with this situation."

"Are they planning to come against us any time soon?" Victor wasn't worried about that. They would get enough of a warning for Bieito to get Kemen out before the army showed up.

"There are murmurs being heard from some of the generals, but so far, as long as we don't kill innocent people, they are content to let us do their job for them." Bieito scowled a little then took a deep breath, relaxing his shoulders. He smiled over at Kemen. "How were your classes today?"

Victor listened to his lover and his son chat while they ate, wishing there was some way to continue sharing moments like these. There wasn't, and at some point in the future, all he'd have left were the memories of how much joy he got from hearing Kemen tease Bieito until Bieito laughed.

There hadn't been enough laughter and joy in his house for so many years — since right after his mother had left. All the sunshine and happiness in his life had disappeared the day she and Pablo had driven away. Oh, he had brief moments with Bieito, but his heart was sore at the thought of all the living they'd missed by continuing their fathers' work.

There was a slim possibility they might have something eventually, but all the work he'd put in had to come to a head. He just hoped Bieito would forgive him for it in the end.

Chapter Eighteen

Mac grabbed his phone, answering it before the ringing woke Tanner. "Guzman," he growled into it as he climbed out of bed.

"The army and DEA are going after Delarosa," Snap told him.

He sat hard on the edge of the mattress. "What? Why? I thought they were content letting him and Cortez fight among themselves."

Snap grunted. "I thought so as well, but apparently, Cortez broke the rules and killed innocents. The Mexican authorities can't ignore that, so they're being forced to raid both compounds."

"Shit." He scrubbed his hand over his hair.

"What's wrong?" Tanner touched his shoulder and he stiffened.

Christ! I don't want to be the one to tell him his brother is either about to die or be arrested. He held up his finger to let Tanner know he'd be a minute.

"Do we know anything else?" He took Tanner's hand in his, holding it tight.

"Not at the moment. I'm at the office, keeping track of shit as best I can from here. The DEA team has been working with the Mexican army on this for a while, so we should know things pretty quickly." Snap fell silent for a few seconds before he said, "I'll call you if I hear anything important."

Meaning he'd call Mac if Victor had been confirmed killed or captured. "Thanks, Snap. I appreciate it."

"Tell Tanner I'm sorry," Snap said softly.

"I will." He hung up then let the phone drop to the carpet when he hung his head.

"They're going after Victor, aren't they?" Tanner's quiet question drifted over his shoulder.

Mac twisted to lie back in bed then he took Tanner in his arms. He pressed a kiss to his temple. "Yeah. The Mexican authorities' hands were finally forced. They had no choice. Snap's keeping tabs on the operation. He said he'd call when he found anything out."

Tanner took a deep breath before snuggling closer to Mac. "Is it bad of me to pray Victor gets away?"

"No, honey. It's not wrong at all. For all the bad he's done in the world, Victor is your brother and you have every right to not want him hurt." Mac trailed his hands over Tanner's spine. "How about I make us some hot chocolate and popcorn? We can watch one of those old horror movies you love."

Neither one of them was going to get any sleep until they knew the outcome of the assault on Victor's compound.

* * * *

The phone Victor was rarely without nowadays vibrated, and he motioned to Bieito that he had to go.

Bieito nodded, not pausing in diagramming the assault they were planning on Cortez's main compound.

He shut himself into his office and moved to the corner, far enough away so no one could overhear his side of the conversation.

"Yes?"

"The army is coming, Mr. Delarosa. You have maybe an hour before they get there."

He hissed at the information. "I appreciate you warning me."

"You pushed them to this, though it wasn't through your own actions. Cortez knew they weren't going to move unless it spilled over into the general public. He had some of his men kill a couple of people who have nothing to do with your war." The man sniffed in disdain. "The bastard has no clue what he's unleashed. They're going to hit him as well."

"No one ever said he was intelligent." Victor stalked over to his desk, pulling open the drawers and yanking out files. "Our deal is still on, right?"

"Of course. You've already provided us with a great amount of useful information. I'm sure you'll have more to give us when you arrive here." His handler sounded confident. "One of my men will be with the squads that attack you. They know what to do. Just don't get shot before they get to you."

Victor grimaced and said, "I'll try not to. Is there anything else I need to do or say? I need to warn my men, so we can start moving the dependents into safer areas. I don't want them injured."

The man snorted. "The best thing for you to do would be to surrender without fighting, but I'm aware that'll never happen."

"Not if I'm to uphold my reputation. You promise no one will find out that I've been an informant?" He'd never had qualms about turning traitor against his father and handing over important details over to certain authorities. It had always been with the understanding that when the time came, the people he worked for would make sure he disappeared.

He wished he'd had a chance to explain it all to Bieito, but he'd had no idea how to broach the subject with him. There was no doubt Bieito would have been angry with him, yet Victor was almost positive Bieito would've helped him if he'd known.

"Of course, no one will know. I keep my word, Mr. Delarosa, and you've never reneged on your end."

"No, I haven't. Remember by giving you the information, I made your career a success. You owe me for that," Victor reminded his handler.

"I do owe you. So do what we planned and you should be fine." The man cleared his throat. "All right. You have an hour. Get your house in order and move who you need away."

"I'll be seeing you soon, I'm sure."

"I can't wait." The call ended.

Victor tossed the phone onto the desk before dashing out of his office, down the hall and skidded into Bieito's.

"All right, gentlemen. The army is on its way here. We have an hour to move all the families out of the line of fire. Get them into the bunkers then take up your positions." Bieito and the others stared at him. "I'm not joking. Bieito, you need to make sure Kemen is out of here. I don't want him in a bunker. He needs to be as far away as we can get him, which means you'll have to take the plane."

Bieito frowned. "What about you?"

"I'm not leaving my men to fight this battle without me. I'm not my father, who ran from any fight like a coward." Victor snapped his fingers at the others. "Go. Do as I ordered. Families and non-essential people need to be in one of the bunkers where they can't be shot accidently. Then make sure the rest of you are armed and take up your places."

The other men raced from the room, calling to people on their radios and phones. Victor had no doubt the whole process would be quick and organized. They ran a drill like this at least once a month. Victor had never had any illusions about how his world would end.

Once they were the only people in the room, he went to Bieito, cupping his face in his hands. He stared up into those beloved brown eyes.

"You must do this, Bieito. You are the only one I trust to keep Kemen safe."

"But you'll be alone. It's my job to protect you. Why can't you come with us?" Bieito gripped his waist, and Victor winced at the strength in his touch. He'd have bruises there for sure.

He shook his head. "Because I won't abandon my people. You know my father would've been the first one on the plane. He never thought those who worked for us were anything other than servants. I think of them as people...some of them as family. I can't abandon them."

Bieito sobbed, his eyes welling with tears. "If I leave, we'll never see each other again. They'll kill you or throw you in prison for the rest of your life. Is that how you want to live? Behind bars and unable to see the sun from your cell? You would be murdered in jail. I wouldn't be there to protect and keep you alive. I would've failed in my job."

"No. Your job isn't to keep me safe anymore. Your job is to make sure Kemen grows into a strong, confident man. You're to see that he falls in love and gets married. He must have children and know the joy of watching them learn about the world." He pushed up onto his toes to press a kiss to Bieito's lips. "You have access to all my legitimate accounts. Let Kemen know it's all his now to do with as he chooses."

He grunted when Bieito wrapped his arms around his waist then crushed him tight to his chest. Victor closed his eyes, breathing deeply the musky scent he'd got used to over the years. Whether Bieito was close by or not, whenever he smelled it, he thought of his lover. He encircled Bieito's shoulders as he was hit with the rather inappropriate wish they had time to make love one last time. He'd love to have one last memory of Bieito's face contorted in the throes of passion and how it felt to claim Bieito in the most primitive way.

Hot tears hit his neck and he realized Bieito shook in his embrace. He wanted to murmur that it would be all right, but he wasn't about to make promises he couldn't back up. Even though he'd been promised certain things, he knew better than to believe a hundred percent in them. Things could change and he could be left out in the cold.

"Come on. There will be time for tears later, Bieito. I need you to be strong and do this one last thing for me." Victor eased away from Bieito, pausing only to swipe the tears from Bieito's cheeks with his thumbs. "Kemen will need you as well."

"What the fuck is going on?" Kemen burst into the room, immediately freezing when he saw Victor and Bieito standing like they were.

Victor stared up at Bieito, silently asking him for his vow, and finally, Bieito nodded. He let his shoulders droop in relief before turning to look at Kemen. *My son. He will be a good man. Bieito will make sure of that.*

He held out his hand, and Kemen came closer to take it. "The army is coming. We only have about forty minutes before they get here. Bieito and you are leaving. There is a plane at the airstrip, fueled and ready for just such a circumstance. Bieito has his pilot's license, so it'll only be the two of you on it. You have to leave now though. I don't want either of you here when the soldiers arrive."

Kemen protested. "No, Father. I don't want to leave you behind." He rounded on Bieito. "How can you agree to this? You love him and you're going to leave him to be killed or arrested."

Victor could see how Kemen's words tore into Bieito as though they were real bullets. He squeezed Kemen's hand hard. "No. Don't punish him for what I've asked him to do. Bieito and you are the two most precious things in my life. You must go together and keep each other safe. That's the only way I'll be able to do any of this." He licked his lips before hugging Kemen. "Promise me you'll take care of him too. He'll need you as much as you'll need him. He's never been anywhere but by my side. Bieito will need you to give him a reason to live without me."

Kemen trembled and Victor grasped how much he'd come to care for him. Somehow in the few days they'd had together, they'd grown to like each other. Maybe there was even some love in there. Yet another thing being cut short he could be angry about later.

"Will you do that for me?" Victor met Kemen's tear-filled gaze.

"Yes, Father." Kemen swallowed hard.

"Good. Then I want you go to pack a small bag. Grab your laptop and cell phone as well. Try not to leave anything behind that might tell them you were here." He gave Kemen a gentle push toward the door. "Meet Bieito at the back door in ten minutes."

Kemen nodded then swung around to run off. When Victor turned back to look at Bieito, he saw his lover standing next to the small safe in the corner of the room. He was pulling files out then stuffing them into two leather briefcases.

"What are those?"

"They're all the files to our legitimate businesses. I don't want the authorities to get their hands on them and freeze the money that's in them." Bieito didn't meet his gaze while he worked.

"Do you have another bag or something?"

Bieito gestured toward a slightly bigger one next to the safe. Victor snatched it up then started tossing stacks of money into it.

"You'll need cash to help establish your new identity. Kemen should be fine. I'm pretty sure no one else has figured out he's related to me, but you will need a new name and background. Use this money to help with that, along with finding a new place in the States to live. See where Kemen might want to transfer to finish up his education." Victor filled the duffle with as many stacks of bills as he could. "You'll never be able to return to Mexico."

"Bieito Perez will disappear from the face of the earth. I'm sure there will be a rumor spread that I died while defending you from the soldiers," Bieito seemed to force the words out.

Victor made a mental note to suggest that to his handler once he met the man. One of the deals he'd made with him was that Bieito was not to be arrested or charged with any crimes he might have committed while working for Victor and the cartel. He wasn't going to allow Bieito to be punished for the things he'd been ordered to do.

"There. You should have more than enough to last for a while without having to touch your own money." Victor closed the bag then slung it over his shoulder. "Come on. Kemen should be ready to leave by now."

Bieito did the same with the two messenger bags he'd been filling, and they took off toward the kitchen. Kemen reached the back door at the same time they did. Victor handed the duffle of money to Kemen.

"Carry this. Now take these, just to get you to the airstrip." He held out two handguns. "Shoot anyone who tries to stop you."

Kemen looked like he was going to protest, but a stern look from Bieito made him take the weapon from Victor. He trailed his gaze over Kemen's face then did the same to Bieito, memorizing their features. Even though people were scurrying around them, he cradled the back of Bieito's head to draw him down for one last kiss. After that, he rested their foreheads together.

"I love you, Bieito Perez. I always have and always will."

Bieito coughed—to cover up a sob, Victor assumed. "Through all the terrible things we've done and all the wonderful moments we've had, I've loved you, Victor Delarosa. I'll love your son like he's my own and I will keep him safe for you."

Victor gave Bieito another hard kiss then pushed him away. "Go now. You don't have much time left."

They took off while he stood in the doorway, watching them leave. Each step Bieito took away from him was a dagger in Victor's heart and soul. For nineteen years, they'd been beside each other through almost every minute of the day. Now they would be alone in a world that hated them.

An explosion sounded from the front of the compound and gunshots rang out. The army had arrived, and it was time for him to pay the piper. He would do his best to defend his people, but he wasn't going to die, not if he could help it.

He saw Bieito stop at the edge of the backyard to look back at him. Victor held up his hand in one last silent goodbye and mouthed 'I love you', then when Bieito had turned away, he whispered, "I'll see you again, Bieito. Whether it's here on earth or in heaven, we will be together again."

Epilogue

Four years later

Bieito stared down at the engine of a nineteen sixty-eight Camaro and sighed. He was going to have to rebuild the whole thing. It was going to cost a pretty penny. He wasn't looking forward to giving the customer the estimate. Yet he didn't doubt the man would pay whatever it cost. He'd seemed rather attached to the car.

After shutting the hood, Bieito wandered toward the back of the garage to where the sinks were located. He needed to wash his hands then head home. He scrubbed but couldn't get all of the oil out from under his nails.

It was a far cry from his old life where he wore designer suits, got manicures and inspired fear in the hearts of evil men. He studied his reflection in the mirror above the sink. His hair was longer, tied back at the nape of his neck with a leather thong. There was more gray in it, to match the deep creases on his face, though aside from a few more wrinkles, his visage hadn't changed over the years. His eyes, on the other hand, had. Where once they'd been cold and had held just a hint of arrogance, now they were filled with sad loneliness.

He blinked. "Stop it," he muttered as he shut off the water. "None of it's important now. You've got one job to do and you'll do it until you die. He trusted you and he might be gone, but that doesn't mean you can break your promise to him."

"Ben?"

While drying his hands on a towel, he turned to yell, "I'm back here, Kemen."

Bieito watched as Victor's son strolled toward him. At twenty-four, Kemen looked exactly like his father—dark-haired and broad-shouldered. Yet Victor had always come across as unapproachable and closed off—mean even, some would say. Bieito had seen that, but he'd been able to look beneath the surface to the man underneath, who was all those things, yet could be so caring when he allowed himself to be.

Kemen's dark eyes held shadows from his time in the hands of the Cortez cartel, but the four years since then had helped to ease the fear a little. He smiled a great deal and was far friendlier than Bieito wanted him to be, yet he wasn't going to stop Kemen from living his life to the fullest. It was what his father would've wanted.

"Did you forget we were going to dinner tonight?" Kemen started to give him a hug.

Bieito held up his hands. "I'm still covered in grime. Let me go upstairs and change. Then you can do all that mushy stuff you seem to like so much." He growled at the younger man.

Kemen laughed. "You don't scare me, old man. Get your ass cleaned up. It's my birthday weekend. You said you'd close the garage, so we're going to hit the beach."

Fuck! He had promised Kemen he'd go to the beach with him. All he really wanted to do was sit in his little apartment and drink all weekend. He dug the keys out of his pocket.

"Lock the place up," he said as he tossed them to Kemen. Once he'd made sure Kemen had caught them, Bieito walked outside to the set of stairs leading to the second floor.

When he'd decided being a mechanic was going to be his new profession, he'd looked around the area surrounding Berkeley, where Kemen had transferred to finish his education. The garage had been on the verge of closing, and the owner had wanted out. Bieito had bought everything—lock, stock and barrel. He'd even kept the employees. It had been a steep learning curve for him, but he'd discovered he actually liked working on cars. Plus, it was one of the few places his enemies—and law enforcement—wouldn't think to look for him.

After taking a fast shower, he changed into jeans, boots and a red T-shirt. He made sure he had his wallet and phone before grabbing a light leather jacket in case it got cool later on. A photo hanging on the wall caught his attention and he stopped in front of it.

Bieito reached out, resting the tips of his fingers on the glass covering Victor's lips. "He's turning into an amazing young man, Victor. I know you'd be proud of him if you were here."

"Ben? Get your butt down here. I'm hungry," Kemen shouted from the bottom of the stairs, and Bieito shook his head.

"Though there are times I'd like to choke the life out of him," he muttered as he turned away from the picture.

Bieito climbed into the passenger side of Kemen's Chevy Cruze and studied the sign over the garage. It still had a new paint look to it. *Ben's Garage.* He was Benedict Cardozo now, born in Portugal to an American father and Portuguese mother.

He'd managed to save his personal fortune and most of Victor's before the DEA had frozen all of the Delarosa accounts. At least Kemen wouldn't have to worry about money the rest of his life. He'd been upset until Bieito had explained that it hadn't been made in the drug trade. The government had taken all of that. What Bieito had gotten his hands on was the legitimate wealth Victor had built up from an inheritance he'd received from his mother's mother. Kemen hadn't been entirely convinced, but he stopped arguing when he'd seen how upset it made Bieito.

"Is it still weird after four years?" Kemen asked softly, as he pulled out of the parking lot.

"Is what?" Bieito didn't really want to talk about it, but he'd learned that Kemen wouldn't let it go until they discussed what the younger man was worried about.

"Your name and working as a mechanic instead of what you used to do." Kemen kept his attention on the road, but Bieito could tell the kid was focused on him. "Knowing there are people out there looking for you. Never being allowed to tell anyone the truth about who you really are."

"Two can keep a secret if one is dead," he muttered.

Kemen shot him a confused frown. "What the hell does that mean?"

"I guess it should be three can keep a secret if one is dead," he stated. "You and I have a pact to never talk about him. It's easy to get lost in the present when the memories of the past are too hard to deal with. Besides, Bieito Perez died while trying to protect Victor Delarosa. At least that's what all the reports say."

Nodding, Kemen seemed to understand what Bieito meant. "I can't say I miss him since I never got to spend any real time with him, but what time I did have with him made me respect him. I still don't like that he was a drug lord."

Bieito patted Kemen on the shoulder. "I understand, and he would've as well. It's why he stayed away from your uncle as much as he could too. He didn't want to compromise any kind of life you were going to build. Unfortunately, circumstances beyond his control brought you into his world and you paid the most."

"I think you were the one who lost the most. I never really had either of my parents. Mother never talked about my father, so I didn't know him. She was too busy trying to find a man who would stay. In the end, it was one of her men who basically gave me over to Cortez." Kemen grimaced as he turned onto the main street.

"I'm sorry." There wasn't much else he could say to that. "I didn't lose anything, really."

Kemen snorted. "You lost the man you loved because you had to save me."

"It was what he wanted." He wasn't going to comment on the whole 'the man you loved' statement. There had only been that one moment at the very end where love had been mentioned. With death imminent, the truth had a way of coming out, yet it wasn't what men like them said. Hell, he wouldn't even have admitted to loving his mother.

"Yeah. I know that." Kemen stayed silent for a few minutes. "I've been seeing someone."

Bieito chuckled, glad that he'd changed the subject. "I know."

After pulling into the restaurant parking lot, Kemen turned the car off then turned to look at Bieito. "You know?"

"I don't invade your privacy, Kemen, but I do keep track of your friends and who you're interested in. While I'm sure no one knows who you are, I can't be too careful that someone might figure it out. Your father wanted me to protect you, and that's what I'm doing." Bieito held up his hand when Kemen began to say something. "Stop. As I said, I don't spy on you. I simply do background checks on the people you surround yourself with to make sure there isn't anything suspicious in their lives. Once I clear them, I don't much care what you do."

"But you know about her?" Kemen climbed out after he asked.

He stepped out then looked around, checking everything out before he motioned Kemen forward. Even after four years, he kept on his toes to ensure Kemen stayed safe. Shaking his head, Kemen led the way into the restaurant.

"Yes, I know about her. I checked her out and, personally, I think she's too good for you." He grinned when Kemen glared at him. "She's a beautiful lady. Do you like her?"

Kemen ducked his head for a second then met his gaze. "I do, but I'm not sure I can keep doing this."

Waiting until after they were seated, Bieito knocked his fist on the table to get Kemen's attention. "Keep doing what?"

"Lying to her about who I really am. Who you really are. I want her to meet you, but you told me I couldn't bring people to see you because it could complicate things. I don't know why. You're my only family, Bieito. I can't take her to see any of the others because they don't even know where we are." Kemen gestured wildly with his hands as he talked.

Bieito listened and smiled. "If you want us to meet, you can bring her over to the apartment for dinner some night."

Shock washed over Kemen's face. "But you said —"

"I know what I said, Kemen, but we can't live our lives hiding away any longer. I'm doing all I can to keep you from getting in trouble with the bad guys." He shrugged. "I can't keep you from living your life. I don't want to lock you away. So bring her over for dinner and I'll meet her. While we can't tell her the truth about your father, you can share some of your life with her. You can tell her I'm your uncle or whatever."

"Can she come to the beach with us this weekend?" He looked so excited.

Chuckling, Bieito nodded. "If she's available."

Kemen shot to his feet. "I'm going to call her right now. Order me my usual."

He watched as Kemen dashed out of the building, tugging out his phone as he went. Bieito laughed softly. Had he ever been so enthusiastic about anything? With a sigh, he thought about Victor. Yes. There had been one person he'd lived for, and every day, no matter what terrible things happened during it, was brighter because he was there.

Closing his eyes, he thought about the last time he'd seen Victor. He'd been dragging Kemen to the airstrip where a plane had waited for him to fly them out of danger while the DEA and the Mexican army had been coming in the front. He'd looked back one last time and Victor had waved at him.

Victor's dark gaze had caught his and he'd seen Victor mouth 'I love you' before he'd swung around to head back into the house. Bieito had known his lover was giving them time to get away by sacrificing himself. He thought he'd have to call their lawyers when he got Kemen to safety, but he was wrong. Somehow Victor had been killed in the altercation.

Bieito never could figure out how Victor's death had happened. He had no doubt that orders had been given to bring Victor in alive. Both the Mexican and American governments would've wanted to make him an example of justice, scaring the other drug cartels.

The first couple of months after the raid, Bieito hadn't slept. Just spent many nights, staring out into the darkness, remembering the years he'd been with Victor. All the dangerous moments and the happy times had run through his mind. It had finally taken Kemen explaining how worried he was about Bieito for him to break out of his depression. He couldn't let Victor down by failing to keep his son safe.

"Damn it," he muttered as he started to reach into his pocket for his handkerchief. Tears welled in his eyes, and he didn't want Kemen to come back to find him crying.

"Here. Use mine."

A pristine white linen square appeared before him, and Bieito looked up to find a handsome older man standing beside the table. Bieito shot to his feet then took the offered item. His throat closed up and he found he couldn't speak.

He'd never seen this man before, but, oh, those dark brown eyes. He saw them in his sleep every night. Those beautiful eyes held all the love in the world just for him.

"Your son seemed quite happy when he raced out of here," the man commented, smiling at Bieito.

"He's not my son. I'm watching over him for a very close friend of mine." He wanted to step closer. Hell, he wanted to throw himself into the man's arms.

"Your friend is a lucky man to have you care so much for him that you would give up your life to take care of his only child." Those eyes told him everything the words couldn't.

Bieito swallowed. His hand shook as he held it out. "I'm the lucky man to have a friend like him. I'm Benedict Cardozo."

Their hands touched and it was as though the entire weight of the world lifted off Bieito's shoulders. The darkness that had haunted him all of those years disappeared under the firmness of the man's grip and the gentle smile on his face. It didn't matter at the moment how he had survived, or why it had taken him four years to come to Bieito. He was alive and there. That was all that mattered.

"I'm Vincent Benes. I've been recovering from an accident and needed a change of scenery, so I thought California would be a nice place to come stay for a while. I came into the restaurant and I saw you were upset. I couldn't let such a handsome man look so sad." Vincent lifted his other hand to cradle Bieito's cheek. "How can I put a smile on your face?"

"You can love me," Bieito said under his breath, knowing no one except Vincent could hear him. "Just love me forever. My life will be complete if you would."

Vincent's face lit up with joy. "I've always loved you, Bieito. You are the only one in my soul."

That was when he was sure. It wasn't just his wishful heart seeing things in a kind man he wanted so badly to see. Victor Delarosa—now Vincent Benes—stood before him and loved him. Bieito's cold and lonesome life had changed in an instant to a truth so honest and enduring, it would last forever.

* * * *

Tanner strolled through the cemetery, letting his mind wander back to conversations he'd had with Victor. He missed his brother so much, even though it had been four years since they'd last talked. Pressing his hand to his chest, he ignored the pain in his heart.

When Snap had brought him the news that Victor was gone, Tanner hadn't believed him. Victor Delarosa had been larger than life. There was no way a mere bullet could kill him, yet Snap had told him there was no doubt Victor was dead.

There hadn't been any body for him to bury, but he'd put up a small headstone by their mother's and visited it once a week. It gave him a chance to talk to Victor like he never had during their lives together.

A bright splash of color caught his attention as he drew closer to the gravesites. He gasped when he saw a bouquet of wild flowers resting against his mother's tombstone. He shot a wild glance around to see if there was someone watching. When he didn't see anyone, he dropped to his knees then drew out the small envelope hidden among the stems.

He tore it open and read the message scrawled in a familiar handwriting.

Be happy, Pablo. We'll meet again.

About the Author

There is beauty in every kind of love, so why not live a life without boundaries? Experiencing everything the world offers fascinates TA and writing about the things that make each of us unique is how she shares those insights. When not writing, TA's watching movies, reading and living life to the fullest.

T.A. Chase loves to hear from readers. You can find her contact information, website details and author profile page at http://www.totallybound.com.

Totally Bound Publishing